HARMATTAN

HARMATTAN

IVAN SRŠEN

Translated from Croatian by
ELLEN ELIAS-BURSAC

Abibiman
Publishing

New York & London

First published in the United Kingdom in 2023 by
Abibiman Publishing
www.abibimanpublishing.com

Copyright © 2023 Ivan Sršen

Abibiman Publishing is registered under
Hudics LLC in the United States and in the United Kingdom.

ISBN: 978-1-7397747-4-5

Cover design by Stephen Embleton

Printed in the United Kingdom by Clays Ltd.

This book is published with financial support by the
Republic of Croatia's Ministry of Culture and Media

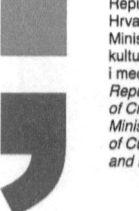

Republika
Hrvatska
Ministarstvo
kulture
i medija
*Republic
of Croatia
Ministry
of Culture
and Media*

Publisher's Note

Ivan Sršen and I met by the strike of a magical thunder. I read somewhere online that he had invited Nobel Laureate, Professor Wole Soyinka to a book fair in Croatia. That, and then, I knew, he was someone I needed to pursue up. And I did. He is married to a Nigerian and he has written a book with Nigerian characters.

I wanted to have it published in English language, so others can read it.

I chased him and got the rights and Ellen agreed to translate it. Then came the financial support of Republic of Croatia's Ministry of Culture and Media.

Now, here is the story and I hope you will enjoy it as much as I did.

Onyeka Nwelue
Publisher, Abibiman Publishing

.1.

The penetrating rumble from the motor of a green police van shattered the utter silence of the quaint little southern German town. The van rocketed through the streets, as if the very sight of the neatly painted three-hundred-year-old buildings and early morning quiet inspired the driver to race. In the back of the van sat three people; two white men and a black woman. The white men were wearing police uniforms and serious facial expressions. During the drive they traded glances, as though checking each other's eyes to see just how much time was left to their shift. The black woman was in civilian clothing, as was the practice for prisoners when they were being transferred. She did not trade glances with the policemen. Instead she focused on seeing as much as she could through the barred windows. Though the scenes of the brightly coloured facades whisked by, the architecture and urban feel suggested that she was in a small town, far from the life she loved. But she felt no fear, long ago she had left fear behind. She even felt a pulse of impatience. What would the new prison be like? Who would she share a cell with? What would the officers and the food be like? Having grown used to the life of a prisoner, she chose to fend off any feelings that might be deemed anticipation in order to concentrate on the task at hand: making a good impression. A good impression on the officers, the social workers, the other inmates, and especially those who were begrudging and malicious. None of this posed much of a challenge for her. She knew these people were not part of her life. They had no way of shaping her fate. All she had to do was be ready to play the game. The game of patience.

.2.

The van slowed to a stop. An older officer, the gate officer who was about to wrap up his night shift at Bad Hallbach prison, opened the door. He exchanged a few words with the policemen at the back of the van, and then, flashing an impersonal smile, after reading the induction document, he announced: 'Uhunoma Ahano'. Uhunoma rose to her feet, stepped out of the van, head bowed, escorted by the two policemen, and strove to keep up with them, matching their stride. During the relatively brief time she had spent in Germany, she had picked up enough of the language to glean that the policemen, to break the silence of the minute-long walk to the large entranceway into the outer building of the prison, were talking about breakfast. The conversation did not, however, last long enough for her to figure out which of them had already eaten and which had not; the gate officer gestured to the fellow from the next shift, who, perched in a guard box protected by bullet-proof glass inside the entranceway, was about to begin keeping watch over the comings and goings, and open the gate to let the group of four into the prison compound. As soon as the gate latched behind them, the two policemen stepped back from Uhunoma, as if they were now at ease, but only while the entry officer filled out the prisoner reception form. One of the two policemen signed the form and then returned to stand next to Uhunoma while the other did the same. The gate officer again smiled impersonally and said: 'Search.' The two policemen led Uhunoma to the first door to the left of the reception area and escorted her into a small holding cell. At the same time a thin female officer entered through another door. Uhunoma knew she was one of the regular officers. The woman was sullen, in her late thirties, with bright green eyes, a big nose, and tightly pressed lips; Uhunoma tried to picture her laughing.

.3.

After her physical and after changing into prison garb, Uhunoma was assigned her cell. As the officer was bringing her up to the third floor of the old but well-maintained building, she began to see a logic to the way the female inmates were housed. The German women were in cells on the ground and first floors, the second floor was for women from Africa, mainly Nigeria, and the third floor was for the other foreign women, most of them European. There were women from the Balkans, Russia, Ukraine and other Slavic countries. This did not seem discriminatory to Uhunoma. It limited the likelihood of misunderstandings and clashes in the cells. But she preferred to avoid placement on the floor with the other women from Nigeria. She dreaded the prying questions, the badgering and jealousy stemming from, if nothing else, the fact that she was a newcomer, while they had already been there for months. When the second-floor officer escorted her up to the third floor she realised she was being placed in the European section. Yet as she was entering the cell, she saw that the woman sitting on the lower bunk was dark-skinned. Perhaps Uhunoma had been too hasty—often her error. She had nothing against people from her country, but in this situation she preferred to keep her distance. They reminded her of everything she could be doing, all she could have had, instead of sitting on a prison bunk. The woman on the lower bunk looked up and asked the officer something in German, at which the officer gave a brief laugh and, leaving Uhunoma there, walked out. The cell door was left unlocked, as it was every day at breakfast; anyone who wanted to walk around the interior of the prison, from one floor of cells to another, could do so in the mornings between six and ten and in the afternoons between one and four. Uhunoma greeted her new cellmate in English and stayed standing by the door. Uhunoma couldn't judge exactly how old the woman might be, though she usually had a good eye for that. But there was one thing she did know as soon as the woman looked up. Her cellmate was Ghanaian.

Uhunoma was not given to hatred. Her parents had always taught her to respect her elders and serve as an example for those who were younger. In Benin City, where she'd grown up, there were all sorts of people, of all faiths and languages, so she was well-versed in the mutual distrust that crops up among people from different groups. She knew about the flower's bulb buried deep underground. From childhood an incident was still etched in her memory when all the Ghanaian merchants became undesirables in Nigeria. She had assumed this incident must have been based on something—intolerance towards a people isn't born overnight. There might well be strong reasons for such things.

Uhunoma had known many Ghanaians before she began her life in prison and sometimes she was surprised by how determined they were. They never left a job partway finished, they never cared for what others thought. All that mattered to them was the outcome. While she stood by the door to the cell she thought—are we not all more or less the same? Yet our vanity prevents us from perceiving the flaws others can see in us. Will I be able to look this woman in the eyes across the divide and share who I am with her?

She knew there was nobody who could help; they'd only make matters worse. The prison governor, the female and male officers, the on-duty doctor, the social workers, the reporters who sometimes showed up to check on whether someone had died due to prison neglect, the representatives of associations for protecting human rights who quaked at the very thought that they might be standing before someone who had stripped those same human rights from another person—none of them could free you. Only a lawyer could, one of those worms wriggling up from the depths of legal documents they never properly understood, psychologists of their own failure—terrorising you with their place in the legal order. But Uhunoma had never hoped for salvation. More than anything, she hoped this new cellmate would welcome her. Because if she didn't, if the older woman chose to withhold her hospitality for the same reasons that had just run through Uhunoma's mind, then the days she spent in this prison would be hell. She realised she hadn't steeled herself enough; she could not be indifferent to the thought that the woman from Ghana might turn her back on her. She could happily eat boiled potatoes chopped up finely and cooked with bacon, she could wear the misshapen clothing stretched out for months by an overweight female inmate, she could stand for hours by a window and stare out through the prison bars, but she could not bear to live in the same four walls with a woman who couldn't abide her. She did not want to be a burden to anyone, nor was she to blame for historical intolerance. Seeing that the woman was still eyeing her, she thought, 'I can do this!', took two steps into the cell and turned to gauge the size of the room where she would be spending so much time.

'Good morning.' Uhunoma heard the words, in

English, behind her, and when she turned she saw a gentle smile playing over the woman's lips. 'New?'

Conversation offers fugitives a sense of shelter, a safe harbour for every person who has been shipwrecked, and a faster way to pass the time in captivity. Uhunoma immediately accepted that the older Ghanaian woman, who introduced herself as Nana, would dictate the pace of their acquaintance and their conversation. After the few opening words they exchanged, she realised the woman before her possessed an air of modesty. Uhunoma couldn't, nor did she desire, to jump to any conclusions about what her cellmate would be like. She also preferred not to foster doubts; after all, ever since she'd come to Europe, she had learned to trust only her own vision of happiness, which had nothing to do with what someone else did, said or thought. She even felt she might be becoming European if she wasn't already. Cut off from communication with her own community, cold in her judgment, restrained, calculating. Her parents would be very surprised to see her now.

'Have any children?' asked Nana.

'No, I do not.' Uhunoma sensed loneliness in the question. She was swept by a strange mix of serenity, because she truly had no offspring, and sadness, because if she did, then someone would be missing her now.

'Nigerian?'

Nana seemed to handle difficult thoughts easily. This reassured Uhunoma so she responded to the question with a greater sincerity.

'Yes. I'm from Benin City. I've been in Europe four years now. I see there are women from my part of the world here. From Benin, I mean.'

'Well I am no good at telling you all apart,' Nana answered quickly. 'But yes, you have some similarities with the women downstairs. I have been in Europe for fourteen years. First I was in Italy and then Germany. Here I lived with a German man but we never married. That would have been too big a problem for him; to live with someone who is undocumented for many men, who, of course, have their documents, does have its appeal. They assume you'd die if they threw you out. Do you think this is cruel? You haven't experienced it? I wasn't hoping for anything. He was not a bad man, he wasn't evil. The whole time he and I both knew I was only passing through, and he was the one, in fact, who was mistaken. Why? Because he assumed I had won the golden ox by living with him. An ox, yes, but golden? Heavens, no!'

Uhunoma threw her belongings onto the upper bunk, because apparently Nana was at home on the lower one. She stood in front of the bed where Nana was sitting, gazed out the cell window, and with the hint of a smile she indicated to Nana that she'd listen if Nana went on with her story. She was pleased she'd staved off the rage and the shame of incarceration and had embarked on a path to tolerance, and, who knows, perhaps friendship.

Nana went on: 'Then I returned to Italy. Italy is a good country. Have you been there? Haven't? No matter. You must have heard about it. The Italians are funny. They always behave as if they want to send you packing, as if you are not welcome. They shove you, look askance your way, avoid you, gossip. But, if you give as good as you get they start falling all over themselves, they court you, shoot you sideways glances. They love being mysterious, but in fact they have nothing to hide. They are like little children. I never felt bad in Italy. I lived for a long time in Siena. It is a small city but beautiful. I'd never seen anything like it in Africa. Germany is a wasteland, barren. Nothing but woods, mountains, and, beyond them, plains, factories and supermarkets. A paradise if you have the money. But Italy is different. Have you ever been to Italy? Ah, I already asked. I assume you haven't, you would have said. But why so quiet? Relax, this isn't your first time in prison, is it? So come on. In Ghana they always used to scare me with prison. Cheat someone in a store, you'll go to prison; hide the truth from your husband, he'll send you to prison; give a policeman too small a bribe, you'll do more time than if you hadn't given him a penny. And you'll be behind bars until someone from your family comes along and pays him the rest. But this prison! This is not a proper prison, it's more like an orphanage. Nothing but orphans from all over the world here. Waiting for their little husbands, their lawyers—now that's something I'd rather not talk about—their kids, I don't know who all they're waiting for. They complain about the food, the clothes, the time to get up and the time for bed. I don't complain. I have a weak heart, but I wouldn't have known this if I hadn't come here. The prison doctor discovered the troubles and now I'm being treated. I even feel more mature than I would expect to be feeling. Here—listen to what I'm saying—here you can only grow old. You are safer in here than on the outside. On the outside there is always some fool asking you to lend him money, and then he calls you and you think he wants to pay you back, but instead he wants to get you into bed. On the outside there will be days when you go hungry. You'll eat, yes, but there is always the worry about what you'll have to eat tomorrow. Here you have your schedule. With all your heart you hope they'll release you, but meanwhile you eat their food, sleep on their beds, and evade their glances. Maybe you can even learn something this way.'

.4.

Uhunoma woke up wondering whether she had dreamed this, or whether Nana really was that talkative. She leaned over the edge of the bed and saw Nana sleeping peacefully on the lower bunk. Waking up in the new cell was not unpleasant. The sorrow was still pulsing somewhere near her temples, but it was no longer a feeling that would sap her strength. And if they deported her to Nigeria, at least she'd see her parents again after so many years. More than half a year had passed since the police caught her without papers. In all her years in Europe, more than ten days never passed without her giving her parents a call, at least for a minute, from a phone booth, with a calling card discarded by someone because there was only half a euro left on it. Now, she hadn't heard their voices for months. One of her friends had surely told them of her arrest, and they knew Europe was not

Nigeria. It was not possible to raise the funds, bribe a judge, and buy a loved one out of jail. What worried her most was that probably nobody knew which prison she was in, since the police had taken her into custody at a bus station in a small town when she was in transit. This is why her parents couldn't send their prayers to where she was. Nevertheless, she trusted in divine assistance. The assistance from God who'd brought her here.

Uhunoma fell back to sleep. When she woke again, nothing had changed. Late afternoon. Nana was still in her bed. Being able to sleep for a long stretch was a blessing. At home in Africa, Uhunoma had always been able to sleep. Never was she bored. She only encountered the notion of boredom when she first came to Europe. If your television breaks down, you're bored; when you are alone, you're bored; and you're bored when you are with someone because you feel like time is slipping away from you. Here in prison she didn't have that feeling. She was closer here to how she'd always felt naturally. That feeling when you know where you are, how you got there, and why. In Europe this feeling quickly melts away. On the street nobody notices anyone, just the occasional Moroccan eyes up your bum, but everyone is used to them so they fit into the general picture as well. In prison, on the other hand, you are beaten down by your lust for freedom, again you feel constraint in your veins and you know you need to defend yourself, survive. On the avenues of Brussels, Berlin, you walk as though you're walking down the pathways of a vast cemetery. You don't exist for them, they don't exist for you. A perfect order. When she lived in Benin City, going back and forth between the market and home, Uhunoma always evaded the glances of jealous women, spiteful old men and curious little girls. She always stopped and chatted with the boy who tanked up the cars of the richer customers at the roadside gas station in return for a tip, and on the way home she'd spurn the flirtation of the taxi drivers on their motorbikes. 'Hey kid, how about a quickie and I drive you home for half the fare?' This breath of the interweaving of human glances, their honourable and dishonourable intentions, she was feeling these inside the prison walls for the first time since leaving Nigeria.

.5.

'Going to supper?' Nana's face was right in front of hers. The older woman was quite short and when she stood up straight, her head barely reached the upper bunk. Uhunoma was still sleepy, but she knew she mustn't miss supper on her first day. She splashed her face over the sink at the back of the cell, next to the toilet.

'It's best to shit in the evening, at night, or early in the morning. Then we're in bed anyway so we can open the window. I'm not in the mood to inhale your smells, and I doubt you want to have to think about how I am digesting the prison food.'

Uhunoma glanced at the toilet and quickly left the cell with Nana, who, after her words of warning, was already on her way down the stairs towards the dining-hall.

'Hey there, girls!' A tall and slender young woman

with long hair dyed a pale blond and done up in a ponytail sat at the table next to Uhunoma and Nana. Uhunoma was surprised by her approach, especially by the way the woman spoke to Nana, who was at least twenty years her senior. The woman immediately started eating and Nana prodded Uhunoma in the ribs and said, 'She is from Yugoslavia.'

'We don't call it Yugoslavia any more. Now we have Slovenia, Croatia, Bosnia and Herzegovina, Serbia, Montenegro and Macedonia. Guess where I am from.'

As if shot from a rifle, Nana declared, 'Macedonia.'

'Wrong. You.' She pointed to Uhunoma.

Surprised, Uhunoma hazarded a guess. 'Don't know. Hungary?'

'Hungary is not a part of ex-Yugoslavia, you idiot. Fine, I see you don't know so I'll tell you: I am from Serbia. Look, there are women here from all those countries; see those two at the table? The nearer one is Ana from Kosovo, and the other is Rina from Macedonia. Both of them are Albanian, but I wager I've lost you completely by now. Doesn't matter, you'll catch on. The one sitting over there...'

'Who is lost?' protested Nana. 'I have been watching you since the day you arrived and I know you are from the Balkans. All of you from there are alike. You look alike, you walk alike, you're all loud-mouthed. Why explain who is who now? I know who is who and who is what. And if I didn't think well of you, you daft cow, I would have already left the table'.

Uhunoma wanted to lower the tensions a little. She disliked needless arguments. 'You speak English so well. Have you lived in England or the United States?'

The woman judged that she hadn't rubbed Nana the wrong way so she went on talking just as loudly. 'No, I studied English at school and listened to rock and roll. That's all you need to learn a language. Anyway, my name is Sonja.' She offered her hand, first to Uhunoma and then to Nana.

Nana added, 'Dear Lord, deliver us from a bone caught in the throat!'

.6.

Back in their cell, Uhunoma and Nana lay on their bunks to digest the German cooking as best they could.

'I think our "priest" will be making his rounds tomorrow,' declared Nana in a derisive tone.

'What? Does he take confession from the Catholics in their cells?' asked Uhunoma.

'No, he's the prison chaplain. They don't have them in other German states any more, but we ended up with one.'

'Okay, but what does he do? Why is he coming tomorrow?'

'Ah, my dear, to ask and expect a full answer means to go after fish with a fishing rod in the dead of night.'

Uhunoma was quickly learning to decipher Nana's answers. There was plenty of time before tomorrow and Uhunoma was curious. She knew that when you have lost your freedom, curiosity is both the sweetest and the most maddening feeling. The sweetest is when you can satisfy it. Someone tells you their secret, you learn from a visitor what happened to the person who was to blame for your time spent between the four walls, or maybe you overheard your cellmate talking in her sleep and caught a few words and from them you build her entire life story. Maddening is when someone won't tell you about what interests you the most just then, and just then Uhunoma was interested in the priest. She assumed he must be Catholic, because this part of Germany was mainly Catholic. Catholic priests weren't unknown to her; in Nigeria she'd known quite a few, and she had attended mass now and then at a Catholic church, because it was close to the home of cousins with whom she'd often stay with for a few weeks. These cousins, an uncle's family, even hung Catholic calendars in their house, and they laughed at Uhunoma when she prayed in tongues. Praying to God in tongues was a particular aspect of the Pentecostal church, widespread in Western Africa: at one point in the prayer, the believer stops saying words in the language of their prayer and goes on addressing God in a 'tongue' that is incomprehensible to Satan and all other impure forces. The 'tongue' is understood by the person praying; Uhunoma's 'tongue' could be called *Uhunomian*. In fact the sounds are not words, because nobody, even the person uttering them, could translate them into an existing language once they've left the speaker's mouth. The 'tongue' includes its own mechanism for self-destruction; as soon as God hears it, it is gone, melting away into the ether. Not a single evil force, let alone a person, will ever be able to decipher it. The Catholics call this mysticism. Members of the Pentecostal flock hold the opposite view: prayer is a necessary part of the day. To skip it is the same as skipping a meal, with the same effect. Doing so won't mean you'll be punished, but you will be hungry with the hunger of your spirit.

'Are you a Christian?' Uhunoma asked Nana.

'Yes, I am but I'm no Catholic. You aren't either, or are you?' said Nana.

'No, I am not, they are boring. I love to sing in church. I love it when someone comes to church to free themselves of evil spirits, to treat an illness.'

'Yes, Catholics don't do that. God probably intended for there to be Catholics and Muslims and Hare Krishnas.'

'And Voodoo.'

'And fools.'

Night was falling outside. Uhunoma felt uneasy, as though troubled dreams awaited her. The cell door had been locked for several hours now and she was beginning to feel that this new space—one she was not yet used to and hadn't accepted as her new home—was weighing on her and oppressing her. Nana had already fallen into a deep sleep—rhythmic snores reached Uhunoma. Tears welled up in her eyes. Yet she had told herself she would not cry.

Her bitterness at succumbing to tears brought on even more tears, until her pillow was wet. Uhunoma sat up, took a deep breath and surveyed the bright side of the situation she found herself in. The woman she was sharing the cell with was not bad and it looked as if the two of them would get along well. The food was not bad. The Nigerian women were on the second floor. And the down sides? She didn't dare think about them. More tears. Why couldn't she be with her parents? Why did she leave Nigeria? Frantically she tried to persuade herself that this was meant to be, that there was a reason for all of it, as there was for everything. But why did the officer smile so callously this morning? Whose side is he on? Is there a reason for him, too? Is there a good reason for his impersonal smile, a rational justification? Does this mean he thinks she belongs here? Or that this is all just a bad dream, like her aunt said: 'Life is a nightmare. When you burn yourself on a hot stew pot where tasty offal is simmering and you feel sharp pain, then you're awake just for a minute. Because pain is wakefulness. Pain is not a dream and pain is not life. We are too fragile to live life as it really is.' As if Uhunoma could feel that pain now. And she knew she wasn't dreaming because she didn't fear the pain. Let them hit her. Let them never release her, let them always feed her potatoes and sausages, let the officers get old alongside her, but there was no greater reason for this. There was no necessity that had brought her to this cell. It could only be human caprice. Supernatural forces are not involved in selecting what is served on the prison menu.

The night above the southern German town was peaceful. Uhunoma dropped off to sleep.

.7.

A new morning. The first morning waking up on her prison bunk. The sound of footsteps. The unlocking of the door. Who wants tea? Water? For pregnant women— milk. The smell of warm milk is disagreeable when you are locked up behind a heavy door. You mostly feel like drinking water. Its lack of flavour and its transparency remind you of untouchability and durability. To drink water at six in the morning on an empty stomach is like strolling along an empty country track at dawn. Not a soul in sight, only a few insects floating silently in the air. The first rays of sunlight already burning your face though the air is not yet baking hot. The distant voices of women who woke up earlier tell you—you are not alone.

If the jobs of prison officers, administration, sentries, and cooks were performed in prisons by robots instead of by people, the prisoners probably wouldn't feel quite so bad. They wouldn't be troubled by the presence of their jailers. The robots would take care of everything. They would do the serving. Even when the officers are tending to your needs, they let you know that here you are serving them. A brusque gesture, faster than it should be, a smaller portion of soup, less than you are allotted, and all of this without courtesy, signals that you must obey; you know you are subservient. Which means that first you have to learn this. If you aren't prepared to, you'll fail the exams until you master the material and pass the test. Nobody cares about your children back home. Your parents might as well stand on their heads. What sort of baby are you when you start whingeing as soon as you reach the old continent, cooking up excuses and shrugging off responsibility? Accept reality! Accept what you have coming to you and do your time! Then maybe your descendants will also wise up!

Nana noticed Uhunoma's despair. 'What's eating you, sister?' she asked, 'You weren't born yesterday, were you. I see you are holding all this at bay. Yet, anyone can go soft and become like an overripe pineapple. You don't care, on the outside you come across as robust and unburned, but inside you moulder. Under your skin you go soft—in the next phase you dry out. And nobody will notice, I know. The outer crust is hard, thank God! But I can tell you one thing: here in prison, and I mean here in

Bavaria or anywhere else, in the United States, Sweden or Japan, we are safe. Remember that! I am not saying this as at random, I want you to think hard about it, and then I want you to have a look at the good-for-nothings on the floor below and tell me whether you want to be like them or have anything in common with them.'

Uhunoma knew what Nana was aiming at; this was about magic, mainly black magic. Once a friend told Uhunoma that her boyfriend, a Dutch man, had asked her to tell him all about black and white magic. She told him in great detail about everything that could be accomplished with magic. How someone could be lured off on the wrong path, convinced they were another person, how a beloved soul could be cured through a mental struggle against the evil that had possessed them. The boyfriend interrupted her and told her that what he was interested in were the effects of black magic. She said that if he was more interested in what it could do to a person, he, too, must be possessed by black magic, because it expanded its power by making people think about it. They never found their way out; they continued to get along, even loved each other as much as was possible with his night job as a security guard and hers as an undocumented cleaner at a hotel. But a Westerner cannot grasp what it means to be buffeted by the winds of evil. They played their game, competed in expressing pride, came up with cruelties and consoled themselves with tenderness, but they did not succumb to evil. All those priests, all the bishops, they probably saw to that. Thinking about good and evil was not a subject for conversation at the marketplace or along the banks of the river. Because it is highly likely that if they had embarked on such a conversation, the arguments would have leaned towards evil. As Uhunoma had heard so often, it's always easier to knock a house down than to raise it up.

'Yes, you are so right,' she answered Nana.

'So hold your head up high, sister. If the Europeans were as weak as the people down there believe they are, a zombie would have already been the head of the European Union years ago. What am I saying? That one must have been a zombie before God decided where to send him!'

The prison officer unlocked the cell door and the morning period for free movement began.

.8.

'Rule number one!' whispered Nana while she stood on the third-floor corridor right next to Uhunoma's shoulder and pretended that all she was doing was looking out at the prison yard through a window. 'Avoid conversations about sex. And when I say "about sex", I am thinking of the real thing, fucking and such. For two reasons: you'll disclose to those scum what you wouldn't even want your sister to know, let alone some troublemaker from Bulgaria; and besides, the more you talk about it, the more you miss it!'

A grin stole over Uhunoma's lips.

'Just you smile,' went on Nana. 'You'll be telling me you shared your previous cell with your boyfriend.'

Uhunoma's face took on a serious expression and she turned to look at a group of German women down the corridor. They seemed peaceful, non-violent. She looked briefly at Nana again—a mutually protective relationship had already started developing between them —and when she read from Nana's expression that this group of unknown women did not present a threat, she proceeded down the corridor.

They were young, between eighteen or nineteen and maybe twenty-five. From the dye on the tips of their hair she could gauge how long each of them had been behind bars. Uhunoma strolled over. One of the girls noticed her and warned the others.

'*Allo, Schwester!*' one of them addressed her first in German, and then continued in unpolished English, 'No offence, but we have trouble telling black faces apart. Still, you look new. Am I right?'

'You are,' Uhunoma accepted the conversation. 'How long have you been here?'

'Ah, don't ask me that. Better to ask: "How long, altogether, have you not been in prison?"'

'Interesting,' answered Uhunoma and skipped to what seemed to her like a less troublesome topic. 'Do you know how I might make a phone call?'

'No,' answered the girl, 'but Marta will.'

'Marta who?'

Hearing Uhunoma's question, the rest of the girls stopped talking and gawked at her.

'Marta can do anything,' said another girl from the group. 'She is the prison chaplain's girlfriend. But what can you give her? What do you have to offer?'

'I have nothing to offer her, but I'm prepared to do anything in return for the phone,' Uhunoma answered, self-assured.

The girls exchanged quick glances and then the first who'd spoken with Uhunoma said, 'Fine, we'll put you in touch with Marta, but don't come crying to us later that we saddled you with problems. You asked for it, *Schwester*!'

Uhunoma thanked them solemnly and went back up the corridor to Nana. 'You're doing well. You only just arrived and you're already going to meet Marta!'

'How do you know what I talked about with them?' Uhunoma was startled.

'I know you want to get in touch with your people. Just watch out and think about what to say when you reach them. They may be thinking you are doing so well that you've forgotten to call. Learn about being "inside", because as things stand, this is all we have left.'

Marta's cell seemed different somehow. It was a prison cell, the same as the others, the same size, but it was full of things: clothing, food, dishes, two separate electric hot plates and several other appliances—a radio, a hair dryer, and a miniature black-and-white television set. But of all the things in the room it was Marta who was the most arresting; the woman weighed nearly 25 stone, tall, obese, in fact so fat that Uhunoma couldn't determine how old she was or what her face had looked like before.

'Hi,' said Uhunoma as she entered the cell.

Marta was sitting on her bed, sorting through a big pile of colourful clothes. 'Hi,' she replied, looking up for barely half a second.

Uhunoma wanted to say what she was there for right away. 'I came to...'

'Wait!' interrupted Marta. In that single word Uhunoma could hear a heavy German accent. 'English bad. Speaking slow.'

Uhunoma understood. She started to speak quite slowly and very loudly, as if addressing an elderly deaf woman and not a foreigner struggling with English: 'I... need... telephone!'

'Eh hey!' shouted Marta even louder. 'I am not... I am not...'

Uhunoma couldn't figure out what was going on. Marta suddenly lurched to her feet. Her whole human mass wobbled and it looked as if the tide was coming in and would swamp and engulf all in its path. Uhunoma stepped back and watched Marta's frenzied efforts; she lifted things, threw them to the other end of the room, raised the bed, the mattress, the night table, and then rummaged through two bags that were arranged one next to the other in the corner of the room by the toilet. Finally she extracted from one of them a yellow booklet that she began to leaf through frantically. Uhunoma realised this was a dictionary. Marta finally stopped on one page.

'I am not... deaf!'

'Fine,' answered Uhunoma, this time almost softly.

'What do you want?' Marta calmed down, sitting back on the bed, which sagged under her.

'I wish to make a telephone call. To Africa.'

'That will be difficult,' Marta said immediately. 'I...' Again she leafed wildly through the dictionary. When she stopped at the entry she'd been looking for she said, .'..I warn you. You do not know that I...' again the dictionary, .'..*kann ich... kann ich...* on your head... *scheissen*!' When she uttered the last words, Marta grimaced as if licking a lemon slice. Uhunoma still did not grasp what Marta was trying to say, until she finally arrived at some sort of formulation, 'I shit you on head!'

Uhunoma accepted this introduction as a necessary demonstration of superiority. 'You will shit on my head. I understand.'

'Yes!' Marta was visually thrilled with Uhunoma's understanding of prison hierarchy. 'Good, good! You good! *Also, du willst nach Afrika telefonieren? Ein Moment.*' Marta flipped the pocket dictionary open. 'You... must go... into town. You have... five euros... to call from... pay telephone.'

Uhunoma knew what Marta was referring to. Twice a week the administration organised a group visit to the closest department store where the prisoners could do their shopping. At the department store there was a pay phone that accepted coins. However, Uhunoma had no money whatsoever so she couldn't be put on the list of those who were going shopping. You could only have money in prison if someone made a payment to your prison account, whether family, friends, your lawyer; Uhunoma had no one so there was no money she could hope for. Only one possibility was left; to ask Marta to organise a payment of five euros into her account. She hadn't yet figured out how to word her request, but Marta had already sniffed it out.

'You want... me lend five euros? You do...' the dictionary again, .'..I say!' Marta slapped her forehead, clearly because she was frustrated at not being able to remember English words. Uhunoma knew these five euros would cost her dearly, but she agreed.

As Uhunoma was leaving the room, Marta pursed her lips and sent her a mocking kiss. In the hallway Uhunoma muttered to herself, 'May God smother you in your own blubber. But only after you lend me the money.'

.9.

Bavaria is traditionally a Catholic province, but Carl Ebermaier was from a Protestant family. It was precisely the radically disciplined Calvinism of his father that had brought him to an act which his entire family had never forgiven him for to this day. On his eighteenth birthday he knocked at the door of the parish office of the Church of St. Michael in Ulm and asked the Catholic parish priest to enrol him on the course to prepare him for the sacrament of Holy Confirmation, his ticket into the largest religious community in the world. Carl, however, was not, perhaps, fully aware that his father's world view was still lighting the path Carl's life was taking. His father always said, 'If you stray, if you stand apart from the crowd, know you must have very strong reasons for doing so, whether you admit this to yourself or not. So, do not deny the extremity of it. Your decision to stray is already in itself a dramatic extreme!' He thought about this now, as a forty-eight-year-old priest of the Jesuit order, having transgressed every single vow and every tenet of the calling he had chosen. He had tried countless times to relativise the meaning of the 'extremity' of his father's exhortation. Would his late father have even been able to understand that his son was serving as the prison chaplain in a federal correctional institution for women, that he was involved in a romantic relationship—if it can be called that—with one of the female inmates, while also having sexual relations at times with other inmates; this latter sounded a shade less accusatory when he tried imagining his father uttering those words. 'The women are every bit as lost as I am. And furthermore, they look forward to leaving this place, while I do not have that drive, which means that I am an even greater prisoner than they are.'

.10.

'Where to, Father?' he was asked by one of the officers when he was about to turn from the central prison area towards the section with the female inmates.

'Ah, confessions, confessions,' replied Father Ebermaier vaguely. Sometimes he was elated at the thought of how his priestly garb gave him the right to erase the line between liberty and incarceration. He knew circumstances had only to shift by a degree, and then he, too, might end up behind bars, but this didn't trouble him; indeed, the insight emboldened him, gave meaning to his search for a justifiable lack of conscience.

'The confessions can wait,' cautioned the officer, at which Father Ebermaier stopped and turned. 'There is a reporter here who wishes to speak to you.'

'Has the reporter cleared this with the governor?', Father Ebermaier asked him, hoping the nosy reporter would first have to go and beard the head governor, allowing him to slip away. In his seven years of service at Bad Hallbach prison he had never spoken with a single competent reporter. All of them were dispatched by their editors, nobody really wanted to learn anything or do their research properly. He already knew what the fool would ask, if he didn't succeed in evading the questions: 'What is the role of faith among the women in prison?' Once when a reporter asked him that, he answered, 'Faith helps the female inmates digest the sometimes indigestible prison food.' And the dolt published it. Incredible.

'Everything has already been agreed with the governor. The reporter specifically asked for you and is waiting for you in room 112. I told you, Father, lighten up with the confessions. Our sinful ladies here won't miss them. And besides, they are all innocence incarnate anyway. Their greatest sin is forgetting to say "excuse me" when they fart.' The officer was pressing Father Ebermaier into a little chat, but Ebermaier was in no mood for one with him or with the reporter so he strode off to room 112 to explain to Mr. Curious that today was a busy day, so why didn't he come back in two weeks at a precisely agreed upon time.

When he arrived at the conference room he was quite startled. A young woman, perhaps in her early thirties, was standing there, leaning against the large conference table. Her short hair, dyed several shades of brown and her unconventional attire were both appealing and entirely out of keeping with the surroundings. She reminded him of an inmate he'd been involved with a year and a half before.

'Hello, Father Ebermaier, Ursula Heinz here!' The reporter introduced herself, clearly pleased with her name.

'What interests you, Ursula Heinz?' He was immediately determined to discredit her. Although he found her attractive enough, the thought of spending the afternoon in conversation about prison protocol did not excite him.

'Your relationship with inmate Marta Piatkowski.'

For a moment Father Ebermaier didn't quite know what to say. But a second later he successfully channelled his incredulity into an effective verbal counterthrust. 'My relationship with inmate Marta Piatkowski is no different from my relationships with all the devout female prisoners in this institution. Your sensationalist attacks on people in uniform no longer have any credence, nor are they of any interest. Write whatever you like, but meanwhile, I have a question for you: what is the nature of your relationship with your editor-in-chief? When he is not pleased with your endlessly mediocre and childish, imbecilic articles do you give him the occasional blow job? Of course a reporter on the job does whatever it takes!'

The reporter observed him for a few seconds and

then stepped back from the table and quickly left the room.

Ebermaier was soon in Marta's cell. 'Where did that stupid reporter come up with her questions about our relationship? This is all because of those idiotic letters of yours! How did you come up with the idea of writing letters to a woman's magazine? Haven't I looked after you? Have I neglected you, or, God forbid, abused you? I am the person who is being abused here!'

Marta said nothing, thereby admitting her mistake. Father Ebermaier came closer and stroked her face. 'Oh, now, I didn't mean it that way. That woman got under my skin. There, that's how it is; everybody uses priests these days for target practice. I know you'll tell them that it isn't true and they'll wing their way back to Munich to the sweet, minimalistic decor of their office, and there they will log into their violet laptop on which, after a little help from Google, they'll come up with a new, scintillating topic. And I, Carl Ebermaier and you, my lovely Marta Piatkowski, will live happily ever after until the day comes when the prison menu changes, meaning, forever!'

With his last sentence he succeeded in coaxing a little smile from Big Marta.

'Where is my favourite shrew now? Come on, if the other girls see you in this condition, you'll lose your influence!'

.11.

'May I speak with the prisoner who arrived here most recently?' Ursula Heinz asked the gate officer, still red in the face from her shock at the priest's insolence.

'Uhunoma Ahano!' said the gate officer from the other side of the bullet-proof glass of his little box, speaking into a microphone, and at the same time pushing a slip of paper with Uhunoma's first and last name on it through the moveable plastic tray.

'Could you call her?' Heinz asked the gate officer.

'What I am calling her for? To go with me to the movies?'

Heinz didn't catch his sarcasm. 'No, could you call her to come down from her cell, I would like a word with her.'

'She is not in her cell right now.'

'How can you tell? Where is she then?'

'How do I know? I don't keep track of the movements of the inmates twenty-four hours a day.'

Heinz was not put off. 'Call her over the public address system. I know you can. If you cook up another excuse, I'll pester you to the end of your shift. I'm a reporter, you know I have the right to do that and there will be a shitstorm if you try to shake me off! And then I'll come back every day.'

'Fine, fine!' the gate officer interrupted her and having turned on the loudspeaker in cell 422, he called Uhunoma to the dining-hall exit door.

"Hey, did you give them your real name?' Nana asked Uhunoma who was paying no attention to the voice addressing them in German over the loudspeaker.

'I did,' said Uhunoma, feeling a twinge of regret. Most of the prisoners, especially the women from Africa who were arrested without documents, never gave their real name and often didn't disclose their nationality either. If you don't give them your real name, they can never identify you, and if they ever arrest you again, you just give them the name you gave them before and it will match the finger prints they took from you after your first arrest. That way you raise a wall between your true identity and your European pursuers; they will never know who you really are and there is not the tiniest likelihood that they can extract any sort of information about you from the African country you hail from because there is no such data. Your nationality should not be divulged. It's much better to claim you come from a country recently devastated by war. According to most European laws, this allows you to remain in the country where you end up, even though undocumented, until the end of the hostilities in 'your' country. In short—the host country will not be able to deport you.

Well, Uhunoma knew all this, yet nevertheless she patiently dictated to the investigating judge her first and last name, provided accurate information about where and when she was born, and all the other details about her family that were required. She was getting tired of the whole charade. But her arrival in prison changed her perspective. The spirits of those who lied improved by the day, because the fools around them did not know who they really were, while the few who had 'bared' their souls slid gradually into depression. Uhunoma knew that between these two categories there was no essential difference, everything was in the mind, but the feeling that every guard knew her real name, the name used by those people she recalled with joy, was beginning to eat at her.

'They're summoning you, silly duck!' clucked Nana who understood what the entry guard was mumbling. 'They are calling you down for an interview, and that means you are a star! First you have to go down, and if you don't want to speak with the representatives of the outside world, you will be asked to sign a statement that this was made possible for you. Will you look at her, your second day here and they're already asking for you, while my lawyer can barely tell the difference between me and the Ethiopians! Better go down and have a chat with them, get a feel for what's happening on the outside, who knows, maybe this will turn out to be some sort of lifesaver. Quickly now!'

Although she had no idea why they were calling her, Uhunoma walked quickly out of their cell and ran down the stairs.

Ursula Heinz eyed her for a long time even after the female officer had brought her into the room where prisoners were interviewed. There were several round tables there with chairs, and the only other people there besides Uhunoma and the reporter were a couple who were sitting at an identical table—a young Greek woman and someone who was probably her lawyer.

'Who are you?' asked Uhunoma.

'A reporter for a Munich magazine,' said Heinz, and pushed her card across the table. At this the guard leaped to her feet. She had been scrutinising every move from no more than two metres away, and she warned the reporter that prisoners were not allowed to be given anything by visitors except chocolate and fizzy drinks from the vending machine at the other end of the room.

'What do you want from me?' Uhunoma tried to maintain her cool, though her hope for a positive shift in her situation was colouring her mood.

'I want us to work together to put Father Ebermaier behind bars.' Heinz didn't waste any time. She was thinking there was a real chance Ebermaier still hadn't had the time to make contact with this most recent arrival and she was right to think so. She was ready to get down to business, before the inmate began imposing conditions and demanding favours in return.

Uhunoma glanced over at the female officer. Either the woman didn't understand English or she agreed with the reporter's intention so pretended she hadn't heard anything. 'But why? I haven't even met the man.'

'It would be better not to meet him. He abuses women.'

'How do you know?'

'I can't tell whether you're pretending to be stupid or you really are. If you're stupid, then up you get and back you go to your cell right now, but if you have a good head on your shoulders, here is what you need to do.'

Uhunoma immediately recognised that the reporter was a manipulator, but she sensed no threat from her. Who knows, maybe something good would actually come out of all this, maybe she'd find it easier to get hold of a decent lawyer, maybe the reporter could send messages for her into the outside world... Uhunoma decided to cooperate, but at the same time she offered her own warning: 'If you try to fuck me over, you'll end up in here with us, and then the priest will cost you your head. Nobody likes being here, and I doubt you are someone who would think of this place as a hotel!'

Uhunoma stood up and nodded to the female guard that she was ready to be escorted out. She was not even going to say goodbye to the reporter. Let the stupid mare know who she was talking with, and let her prepare for what would be a collaboration, not one-sided exploitation.

.12.

'Watch out, I think you're not going to get anywhere by becoming a spy for someone on the outside. I'd understand it if this were the police or a court and they offered you a deal. But this way you'll be saddling yourself with trouble beyond your wildest dreams,' warned Nana when they were locked back up in their cell that evening.

'What would you do in my place?' asked Uhunoma.

'I am not in your place.'

Uhunoma liked the way Nana stopped her, wordless, in her tracks. She wielded classic maternal verbal superiority. This was how she knew Nana had children. How many? That made no difference. Nana had decided to treat Uhunoma like her little girl and now, as she was thinking about it for the first time, this deeply touched Uhunoma. How is it that far away from home in the barren hinterland of provincial Europe, at the nadir of your existential amplitude, a woman appears and, with a single word or gesture, raises you above the clouds of your despondency once more? Although Nana had just warned her to avoid anything that would make her stand out in a crowd, the very tone with which she did this filled Uhunoma with a burst of self-confidence. A boxing ring. Prison is a ring. The competitors enter the ring one by one and each goes for as many rounds as the court has set for her to fight. The judge finally declares the victor based on points, and the victor is, always, destiny; a destiny you stubbornly spar with and which, in the end, throws up its arm victoriously while you retreat into your corner. And even worse is when destiny knocks you out—sometimes, for good.

'Fine, I get the point of your sermon. So now, tell me what would you want from the outside?'

Uhunoma's question startled Nana. 'What do you mean, what would I want? We're nowhere near Christmas or my birthday, and the death sentence, as far as I know, is no longer a viable option in Germany. In fact only in the case of this last would I believe that someone in this pit could truly give me what I desire.'

'I'll blackmail the reporter,' Uhunoma answered, calmly. 'She's poking her nose in where it doesn't belong, she is all arrogance and envy—hey, I can see in her eyes that she envies us because of what we are going through here. So she can at least treat us royally for a time, if she can't actually join us.'

'What a twat,' said Nana with a wry smile.

'And who is this Father Ebermaier anyway?' mused Uhunoma, mostly to herself.

As if the guards had heard what they were saying, the loudspeaker stirred and barked: 'Chaplain Ebermaier making the rounds!' Not five minutes later, Ebermaier was already knocking on the door of Nana's and Uhunoma's cell. He didn't wait for their answer, but strode in confidently with the obligatory 'Laus Deo', and then stood in the middle of the cell and looked back and forth between Nana and Uhunoma. Nana turned to face the wall on her bunk.

'Have you decided to come back to the Catholic Church?' Ebermaier asked Nana in a stern tone.

'Listen, Uhi, this lad here has a nasty sense of humour. He has been after me to return to a "Catholic Church" which I never left. And I never left it because my parents never enrolled me in the first place—thank you Dad, you had enough nous not to send me to the Catholic school even though you drank a lot. So I never had to leave and, Ebermaier'—now for the first time, turning around, she looked over at the priest—'you definitely cannot enrol me in it again. Try winning over this little bird instead!' and she pointed at Uhunoma.

Ebermaier calmly turned his back on Nana and stood up to Uhunoma's bunk. He leaned on the edge of the mattress and looked up at Uhunoma. She felt the agreeable disquiet of his male presence, but at the same time she couldn't avoid Nana's reproachful look and the grimace of disgust on her face behind the priest's back.

'Although I know your cellmate has two pairs of ears and misses nothing, I'll pretend that our conversation is confidential. Of course, you won't be speaking to that slut of a reporter again. In fact you will never meet with her again. As far as making phone calls to Africa, you can forget that until you become a citizen of the European Union, in other words—never!'

Uhunoma instantly lost all the momentum that had been propelling her through the last day and a half, and if she hadn't been lying down, she probably would have sunk to the floor out of sheer weakness.

'Fuck off, Ebermaier!' Nana jumped in, to ease the first real shock of the new penitentiary for Uhunoma.

'For you there will be no more privileges, old woman!' the priest was momentarily caught short by Nana's interjection so he watched Uhunoma's bugging eyes, while Nana immediately shot back.

'Since when have I enjoyed privileges, you miserable excuse of a man. *Hohler Kopf, grosser Bauch, kleiner Schwanz*'.

Ebermaier was clearly upset by Nana's last sentence

so he chose to stop his conversation with Uhunoma, turned around and went to the door.

'You will repent of your sins!' he snarled at Nana in passing.

'I am not interested in you!'

Uhunoma wept, or rather sobbed into her pillow, trying to smother her cries. Nana decided it best to let her have a good cry, because here at the worst moments it's best to pull yourself together on your own. If she had been able to tolerate slimy Ebermaier a little better, perhaps she would have let him 'massage' Uhunoma to the end, and that would be her first and last lesson.

'Why did you do that?' Uhunoma suddenly cried out, still through tears.

'What?' Nana could not believe that Uhunoma was protesting her effective defence which had had a clear impact on Ebermaier.

'What do you mean, "what"? You destroyed my one chance of getting in touch with my parents, my one chance to reach anyone by phone! All you had to do was leave him to babble on a bit, and then I'd easily have handled him, won him over. You women from Ghana think you're so clever, and that's why you're still here! Yes, exactly, because you never know how to help yourself!'

After a few seconds of musing on this in silence, Nana said: 'Ebermaier is a nobody. I'll set up that phone call for you. Come on, stop crying...'

.13.

At supper, Nana, Uhunoma and Sonja from Serbia sat quietly around the table and ate. Sonja could tell that something wasn't quite right between the two cellmates so she asked Uhunoma: 'Is this old lady giving you a hard time?'

Before Uhunoma had the chance to come up with an answer which would, of course, have let Sonja know that she was not in the mood for conversation, yet would say not a word about the reasons for the silence, Nana barged in with.

'I may be an old lady, but I am looking after this little newbie,' and she pointed at Uhunoma, sitting next to her.

Uhunoma let slip a smile. She was about to speak but her eyes filled with tears, so all she could do was mumble something. At that point Sonja jumped in, seeing there was a possibility of renewing what was at the very least a charming bond between the Ghanaian and Nigerian women: 'Come on now, old girl, hold on, our generation has crossed half the world on our feet, and our heads hold at least twice as much as your geriatrics do. But I'll admit one thing, you are even quicker with your tongue than the Romanian women here, more power to you!'

Then Big Marta's bottom brushed up against their table and the conversation turned surreptitiously to Ebermaier and his lover. Unexpectedly Uhunoma roamed in her thoughts far beyond the prison dining-hall. There was the door to her family home in Benin City, the building where her parents lived on the first floor with their five small children; she was the third. She could hear her mother's noise coming down from the floor above, Father wasn't home, he was at work. All of them worked, to be fair, except her younger brother who was barely two and had only taken his first steps. Uhunoma's job was selling drinking water in little plastic sachets, and the customers were the passers-by, the people who lived on their street. Here and there someone would buy the little sachet of water for a few cents, or others just patted her on the face or hair and went on their way without buying anything. She had no toys but she didn't miss them, she played all day with the neighbour's son who was just a little older than she was and proud that he was already attending school. They pretended they were seeking the car he had parked somewhere, and the boy always said: 'What a car, what a car!' Uhunoma enjoyed this and they hid until dusk among the low buildings, scampering along the bumpy, unpaved side roads and paths, calmly accepting the inevitability of the end of their game as the last rays of daylight waned. Because there were no street lights where she lived. Street lights on at night had thrown her off at first in Europe, kept her awake at night. You keep waking up in the middle of the night, thinking morning had already come, or lost in the throes of a nightmare you think twilight is only just descending... When you finally get accustomed to unending day, you cease to care whether you go to bed or wake up at midnight, eat dinner at eight in the morning or eight at night, life becomes a monotonous spending of time, or its too speedy passage. And here in prison, you can't help but noticing that Europe also recognises day and night. It dictates life by day and rest by night, the world is the same no matter where a person goes, and all this brings you back to the realisation that you are not prepared for the true taste of survival, you cannot bear it, you think, once you try it all will change, you'll have nowhere to go back to, and indeed this is the case, things are as they seem to be, nowhere have you been mistaken. So sleep, sleep through all the deadly thoughts and wake up prepared for—death.

.14.

'What do you like remembering most?' Uhunoma asked
Nana a little naively, right before bed.

Nana didn't stop long to think: 'I make an effort to
have nice memories only from prison. Understand?'

Dreams in prison have a special weight, some might call
it charm. They become astonishingly realistic, almost
tangible. They tell you how close you are to the unreal
by growing more and more real. The longer you are
behind bars, the more you cherish the time you spend
sleeping. It is not true that all dreams flash through
the mind during just a few seconds of sleep, right
after consciousness has descended to the cellars of the
mind. Dream is consciousness. Dreams follow our path
through the labyrinths of the unconscious. Nothing
there is fabricated. A dream is an unedited documentary;

personality is sometimes what is behind the camera, sometimes it's the ego, sometimes the conscience, but the camera always records only what is standing before it and your sense of self. So when your physical being finds itself in bondage, the camera follows your sense of self right to the front line, albeit reluctantly, where natural forces such as gravity often lose the battle and infinite realms suddenly crack open through which to fly or dive, you can run or walk through them, you could even make your home there, but no piece of this realer than unreal terra infirma can be brought back to reality. That would simply be too much.

Uhunoma sleeps and dreams of her father. Father is leaving the house and getting into the passenger seat of an army jeep. He was indeed a soldier, now retired, but the dream is about a past—though imperfect—time. A white man is at the wheel of the jeep. An extremely unusual sight in the Nigerian army. The white man says something to Father, but Uhunoma can't figure out what it is about. Father nods but his eyes are fixed on Uhunoma. She feels awkward, senses trouble coming and wants to get out of there, to run away. And before she manages to turn she sees the white man say something to Father and then he gets down off the jeep, stands in front of Father who is still sitting in the car, takes the pistol from the holster at his belt and hands it to Father who takes it reluctantly. Uhunoma now can no longer leave;

she is troubled by the feeling that something terrible is about to happen. She shouts to Father to leave the pistol. The white man moves away from the jeep, spreads his hands and says something: 'Fire!' Uhunoma covers her ears, she hears a shot and the white man falls to the ground. Father doesn't say anything, he puts the pistol away in the glove compartment on the dashboard, starts the car and, with a gentle smile, drives away from their street. Uhunoma is standing in front of the house where she was born; nobody there except the dead man on the dirt road. She opened her eyes slowly, as if she hadn't been dreaming, and whispered: 'Thank you, Father'.

'Today we're going to learn about the glorious past of our praiseworthy Kingdom of Benin! *Oba o togbe!'* The teacher almost shouted this last sentence. The children answered:

'*Ise!'*

'How many of you here speak Edo? Raise your hands.' About two thirds of the class either spoke or at least understood Edo. The remaining third were somehow disheartened at that moment, they tried, even though they were nine-year-olds, to give the impression that they were really interested in what was coming. Uhunoma was in the majority. She had been used to living with people, ever since she could remember, who did not speak her native language, and she was quite adept at the Pidgin English that a good part of Western Africa used for communicating. But instruction at school went on in grammatically correct literary English which, from the perspective of a child, might seem like yet another language to learn.

So in this trilateral situation, every day there were many other languages interwoven for the third of the group who used yet another language or dialect—Yoruba, Hausa, Igbo, Esan, Calabar...

The teacher waited for the children to comment on the fact that their class was made up of members of different nations, tribes, groups, and then, in a solemn tone, he got down to business: 'All of you, one day, will serve God by living the life He has chosen for you. Also, you must know that you have already been chosen by God to live in Benin City. This ancient city, as old as Jerusalem, has also been God's city. This is a place that has always been ruled by piety, virtue and righteousness. Jesus Christ has saved us all and he will return again to save us, when the time for this comes, here, on the streets of Benin City, and we must prepare eagerly for this day. How will we prepare for this day? By earnest studying, humility, prayer just as Jesus prayed for us!'

'Amen!' shouted the pupils in unison.

'Teacher!' Uhunoma's thin but ringing childish voice echoed suddenly through the entire classroom, a large room in the one-storey building with earthen walls:

'My daddy says that once long ago in Benin City people killed one another for the glory of God. God demanded that someone must die for him. And as nobody wanted to die for God, they always had to kill someone. Will we have to die for God?'

The teacher assumed a deathly serious expression and walked slowly over to Uhunoma's desk. Then he dropped his chin to his chest and strolled in a circle around the classroom until he sat at the teacher's desk. Once there, he started to tell his story in an almost conspiratorial tone: 'Long before our Lord Jesus Christ arrived on Earth there was Osalobua. Osalobua created all there is, everything came from him. Osalobua had his helpers—the Ehi. Each Ehi was in charge of one person. The Ehi's task was to remind the person of the life he had chosen before he was born in his current body. If the person obeyed his Ehi, he would fare well, if not, nothing would go right for him. But people thought they could address Osalobua directly so they began to bring him sacrifices. First a few necklaces, then animal flesh, yams, and finally they resolved to sacrifice people, not knowing that as long as they weren't listening to what their Ehi were telling them, all this was in vain. That is why Jesus Christ came down among us, ordered people to stop sacrificing one another for their aspirations and reconciled us to our fate. And that, children, is why we are Christians'.

'He is a Muslim!' a little girl pointed at the boy sitting next to her.

'I still have my Ehi, he stayed on Earth even after Christ came. Daddy said they are both going to watch over me,' said Uhunoma, although nobody was listening to her any longer because of the noise that had spread across the classroom as soon as the teacher stopped speaking.

.15.

'Lazybones,' hissed Nana.

Uhunoma shivered and sat up in bed as if something had struck her.

'Do you understand that a new day has dawned and you must accept this? You need to forget what was in Africa, you must forget what was in Europe, you must forget what was in Germany before they caught you. Why did they catch you? That you must also forget! What were you dreaming last night? Erase it from your memory!'

'What should I do about that reporter?' asked Uhunoma, still groggy from her afternoon nap.

'I don't know, get in touch with her, ask her for help. She won't be able to help you, but now she cannot hold you back either. The damage is done, you fucked up, Ebermaier has his eyes on you, Big Marta is no longer an option, well, maybe it really is better for you to slam every door shut, that way you'll find peace sooner and cleanse yourself of the rage.'

'What rage?' asked Uhunoma, mostly to herself.

'The rage of a trapped animal' said Nana calmly. She sat on her bunk, pulled a magazine out from under the mattress, and began to leaf through it.

'What's that?' Uhunoma was intrigued by how Nana spent her 'free' time.

'A German magazine for men—models and that sort of thing. I'll lend it to you later, it will do you good, only that I have no intention of becoming a lesbian and I'm not keen on having my cellmate pinching my bum in the middle of the night!'

Bleak is the fate of those who have no one. This was the thought that could bring Uhunoma back from the darkest depths of her despair. But it was like a brief hit, and then, after the flashes of ecstasy, she'd feel herself slipping back into a reality which, on this question, never deceived itself, in fact it always seared like an open wound. Prison allowed her to eliminate from her mental environment people she didn't like; a peacetime republic was created in her mind of undisturbed social relations and connections, equal participants in her emotional life. It was remarkable how quickly she succeeded, perhaps by following Nana's strict instructions, in jettisoning from her contemplative discourse most of what had oppressed her while she was still at liberty on the outside. With each new day she learned to bear with greater ease that single, vast, indeed gigantic, weight, that all the female inmates dragged along with them, the weight of life under lock and key, until, after a time, it turned into something more like a bulwark. What interest rates are for the banker, the field for the farmer, and the cover of night for the criminal, cells are for prisoners. The cell is their activity: when a schoolchild has had enough of sitting at their school desk, the classroom cannot prevent them from walking out the door. The same holds true for the office of a clerk who is unhappy with his job, or the retiree upset about the daily meals provided for them—convinced that the staff at their retirement home are systematically poisoning them. If we give our imaginations free rein, the freedom they enjoy could be said to engender paranoia. In prison there is no paranoia. If something ugly is in the works for you, you'll feel the consequences so quickly that nothing is left up to your judgement. In prison you are stripped of the right to predict. You can read the future in cards, you can dream, but the essential, highly irrational planning for the future of a person who is at liberty is not an option for you. You were not given access to utopia, the dogs of vulgarity were set on you.

.16.

Ursula Heinz hadn't had many enemies in her life. She'd knocked heads with a fellow reporter over divergent world views, sometimes only over male–female frictions, as she herself called them. As far as Ursula was concerned, falling in love, flirting, coquetry, teasing were all baseless euphemisms for 'friction'. Frictions happened between two people when they felt a sexual charge. As sex is a game of both subordination and domination, friction happens when the people taking part send like signals. Subordination and subordination, or domination and domination result in sparks, or friction. Friction that will probably ignite a blaze rather than fuse two compatible impulses—domination and subordination. When compatible impulses are fused, the participants in the interaction most often caress each other with looks, exchange a few nice words, and continue on their way.

'Friction' regularly results in some form of physical or emotional bond.

Ursula was satisfied with the material she had collected for the article for the next issue of the Munich women's magazine *Kumpanin*. With this thought she was back again at the gate officer's box at Bad Hallbach prison, requesting a conversation with Uhunoma.

After slightly more than half an hour, Uhunoma appeared in the visiting area, which was almost full to the last seat with inmates and their families, friends, lovers, husbands.

'You again,' asked Uhunoma, by now armed with a well-worked out plan. 'Why?'

'Listen', Ursula said in a serious tone in clear English with a pronounced German accent. 'If you want to make a trade, go ahead and tell me what you want, but you'll have to be realistic. I am not a billionaire nor am I a justice on the highest German court. I believe you're cleverer than you let on, but feel free to vent to me and explain how we German women and other white European women have no idea what it's like to come to Germany to slave away and then be kicked in the arse and sent back to your African womb.'

Uhunoma thought about whether the reporter was reaching for freer, more insulting language on purpose, or was simply using the English she had learned at school. Interesting how this stranger was making this effort about such positive things: she seemed interested in informing ignorant German women about the imperilled rights of certain groups of neglected women, while meanwhile offering to do her a favour of her choice, and all this would be a stab in the prison administration's back, and, sweeter still, in Ebermaier's. Why had she never thought that journalism could show such a positive face while she was living in Nigeria? Reporters, for her, were scavengers who photographed the mutilated bodies after a traffic pileup on the Lagos–Benin City motorway, never giving a second thought to helping the accident victims who were half-dead, their limbs severed and crushed, calling out to their children trapped under the wreckage. Or they were the brown-nosers currying favour with the powerful local and federal politicians, competing to see who would take the picture of a power-monger in the most fetching pose, as if the overweight thugs in suits stepping out of the black Mercedes had suddenly turned into tall, slender models, the figureheads of fashion houses and the costliest perfumes.

And on top of that, in Nigeria you might occasionally see a female reporter, but they were sure to be the mayor's mistress or some sort of mystical, bejewelled figure who remained sitting in the black air-conditioned limousine and never showed her face. She remembered one female reporter who came from Lagos to write about the theft of construction material during the building of the Benin

City–Onitcha motorway, but that was many years ago. They all saw her limping slowly one morning, leaning on a cane, from the construction site to the centre of Benin City, literally dragging her broken leg along the ground. After that there wasn't a single reporter willing to come from Lagos to poke around on government building sites from which from one year to the next everyone brazenly helped themselves to material of all kinds, while of course the supervisors took their generous cut, and the supervisors of the supervisors took theirs, as did the big bosses, and on and on...

Why was Ursula Heinz willing to give so much, yet take so little or almost nothing in return? In return all she would be given was a pure lie, a fabricated story about suffering for the entertainment of Munich housewives. Uhunoma knew that maintaining a lie is always the purest and safest thing to do. A lie is sterile. It sticks you, like a hospital needle, where it is supposed to and has no side effects. It injects the necessary serum for those who long for it. A lie is also easiest to control: it spurs the imagination and fosters creativity; we spread the limits of our possibilities with it, we step into the new, acting as screenwriter, director, and leading actor in the process, and the outcome of the plot is known to us in every detail. What about the truth? The pestilential matter, truth, rots under the surface like gangrene, while the person who has uttered it is turned on the spit of consequences, stripped of any method of extricating themselves from the damned position they have worked themselves into. But once you have uttered a lie—right up to the moment when you speak the truth—your word will be taken as the law etched in stone, serving as an example for consistency; the human mind is poor at remembering and registers words not as they are spoken, but as it would prefer to register them. So if you keep at it, you'll make your lie more pliable than any rigid and tedious truth that has only one quality: it can destroy anyone who places their trust in it.

Uhunoma felt as if she were conquering territory, which is probably exactly how the reporter wanted her to feel. At the same moment she thought of Nana and was appalled when she could almost hear in her head Nana's arguments against any sort of action, sentences that Nana had most probably never said to her, yet now they had formed in Uhunoma's mind as a warning: 'You'll start the ball rolling and you won't be able to stop it. Give up on the fervour of the moment and learn to live with your imperfections. Only those who do not yet feel pain are prepared to plunge into pain.'

'Do you have any children?'

'I do not and I don't see why that is important,' answered Ursula.

'It is important because it means that you have no one to miss you,' Uhunoma looked Ursula in the eyes.

'You have pretty eyes,' said Ursula quickly. She was beginning to feel a certain awkwardness and had already forgotten half of the key elements of help she needed to pursue her strategy in acquiring Uhunoma's side of the prison story.

'I don't go with women,' Uhunoma told her. 'Just so you know. That is what least interests me right now.'

Ursula was embarrassed, and that was what Uhunoma was aiming for. Let's see what is behind that cloak of fearlessness!

'No, you didn't understand me properly... Perhaps I'm mistaken? Please, forgive me if in your culture women do not address each other in this way...'

Uhunoma couldn't restrain her smile and this was her first positive experience that day. So she decided to bring the reporter in a little closer, telling her what was in her heart: 'You fool, the women I know massage each others' breasts and bottoms, no problem. What the fuck's wrong with you? Listen, you come here from the outside and start hustling me, what else am I to think? That when I've had enough of this conversation I can get up, walk out of this building, and go to the closest café in town to light up a cigarette? In case you didn't know, we are not allowed to. So show a little consideration. Your offers mean nothing to me, nothing!'

Uhunoma didn't raise her voice much nor did she frown. She thought, if a reporter can't take a frank conversation, why waste my time on her?

Ursula didn't know how to go from there, but her journalistic instinct nudged her to say something.

'Fuck you, you cow!' blurted Ursula.

'Oh, well done you! And fuck you and your ugly make-up and horrible boots!'

Ursula's eyes filled with tears and she would have started crying if she hadn't bitten her lip. She stood up from the table and shot like an arrow out of the visiting area. Uhunoma knew the reporter would be back. She leaned on the hard arm of the prison chair, linked her hands behind her head, relishing the unpredictability. A phone conversation with home quickly took shape in her mind—she'd tell them all about this. The conversation was still a possibility. Her mood sank again when she faced the fact that Nana was always right.

Ursula banged on the windowpane of the entry guard's box when she was brought there by the guards.

'Open the door, you fucking bastards. I am not a prisoner here, come on, faster, hear me?'

The gate officer dragged his heels in attending to her, retrieving her prison pass. As she was walking out into the fresh air she tried to remember why she had set out to write a story about Bad Hallbach women's prison in the first place. Nothing came to mind. She went out the front door of the prison complex and over to her sleekly scaled-down version of an off-road vehicle. She took off her narrow leather jacket and tossed it into the boot, loosened her hair and sat behind the wheel. She felt like when Ralph, the cute sixth-former from her school, slept with her and then boasted about it to the everyone there the very next day. 'Why don't I feel sorry for the women in prison?' she wondered.

.17.

There weren't many chances to walk around the prison yard, especially not on colder days, and the days here never seemed to stop being cold. They lasted like time that never began and never would end: none of that exists and when you wonder what you are thinking about you realise you are merely—wasting time. 'It's great to be alive,' thought Uhunoma as she paced over the hard, well-trodden ground that gave no sign of grass. Though the yard was very small, still they could see the bright sky, hear the screeching of birds, feel warm food digesting in their bellies, as one of her many flatmates explained to her soon after she arrived in Europe : 'Just you take your chances, eating canned fish and cold pasta from the fridge. Eat warm food here or you'll be done for within the year.'

Nana spat on the floor in the corner of the yard

where she, Uhunoma and Sonja had stopped after walking a few laps.

'Lovie dovies, now your auntie Nana will tell you a few things that matter.' Nana was talking as she climbed up onto the rusty remnant of bulky iron gym equipment that had been left outside. 'You, my girls, are representatives of world poverty. When I see you it is like I'm seeing the beggars on the streets of Accra.'

'Hold on a minute, Grandma,' interrupted Sonja, 'so maybe I deserve being teased, but don't you be going after Uhi, you know such things hit her hard.'

'Look, you two don't understand much. Tell me, how can you learn something if you think you're the cleverest of them all?' Nana assumed a stern expression and crossed her arms, 'Do you think you'll convince yourself that you're fine and that you are God's chosen one from head to toe?'

'I don't give a fuck for deities. I'd sell my soul to the devil like Robert Johnson if I knew my music would change humankind,' said Sonja, rubbing her hands together importantly and blowing into her fists from time to time to warm up her frozen fingers.

'Who's that?' shot back Nana.

'An American blues musician, you ought to know that. Didn't all black Americans come from Africa?' Sonja jammed her hands into her pockets and held her last remaining cigarette in her teeth though she wasn't planning to smoke it.

'I don't know any John Robertson or any other American jazz musicians... There, little girl, you think that because I'm from Ghana I should know the names of all the American chancers. And, if I heard right, you said he is black? Is he, now, and I thought the only people living in the United States were the cowboys and the Indians! Come on, kiddo, go to sleep and let me know when you are old enough to be weaned from your mother's breast.'

Sonja wasn't about to be put off, she wanted to explain to Nana her own view of the world: 'Hey, old woman, rock 'n roll is my way of life. I survived the worst years in my country because I didn't listen to what my parents, teachers and anyone else were always going on about, like you now. I believe in love, right Uhi?' Sonja was looking for an ally in her appealing little spat with this woman who was old enough to be her mother.

Uhunoma didn't want to play. She didn't know what she could have said. Still, she asked Sonja: 'How did rock 'n roll help you in life?'

'Well it didn't do much for her. She's here with us today!' interjected Nana.

'Laugh if you like, but this here is something, compared to what I had at home,' said Sonja in a conciliatory tone.

'That's what I'm saying to you,' said Nana, 'but you won't let me finish. You and Uhi come from the blackest of black holes of the world.'

Sonja interrupted Nana again, this time with peals of laughter. Then with one arm she hugged Uhunoma, drew her close and straightened up into an unnaturally stiff posture as if Nana were summoning them to a bizarre parade.

'Yes, yes, go ahead and laugh, you ignoramuses, blessed may you be in your ignorance. The point is that this is our natural environment. We cannot go beyond this. This place is the furthest we'll get. Enjoy it all, because this is our swan song.'

'Fucking hell, old woman, you'll do us in with these stories,' sighed Sonja.

.18.

The three dubious women were approached by a prisoner none of them knew. In very choppy English she said: 'I ask to hear about what you are so laughing.'

'Knowledge is too strong a poison for you, my dear!' Nana said through laughter. 'Where did you come from, and what business is it of yours, what we are talking about? Come on, scram!'

'Wait,' said Sonja, 'this bird might just be one of our flock.'

'Mine she most certainly is not, but if she's yours, take her, we won't stop you, right Uhi?' Nana was still on a roll.

'No, no, I don't mean it that way, I believe she and I come from the same... tribe.'

'Ohh, well fuck me,' Nana was unusually radiant. The unknown guest left, a little insulted. 'That's all we need, some hussy from a Balkan tribe who will entertain us until the wee hours! I am tolerant, if you insist on socialising along blood lines, be my guest, but first tell her to brush her teeth and scrub her tongue, because you moustachioed models, reek of garlic. I often wonder whether you are served a special Balkan menu here. Thank goodness, if you do, because I don't even want to know how to find that food, let alone try it. The Pakistanis are babes in arms compared to you, your mothers must bathe you in garlic from birth!'

'Uhi, will you listen to our chubby Ghanaian's speech! She doesn't like garlic, as if she'll die of it, and as if this prison is her royal flat and all the rest of us are the cleaning staff at a five-star hotel!' Sonja was just getting going, and was reaching for even more stinging insults.

A sincere grin slid over Nana's face: 'Come on, call that tribeswoman of yours over here for us to work her over a little, and see whether she's up to snuff, eh?'

Sonja embraced the reconciliation offered to her and went after the woman who had already slipped off to the other side of the yard. Uhunoma went after her, she didn't want Nana commenting on Sonja's behaviour behind Sonja's back.

'Do you see her?' she asked Sonja.

'There she is, by the wall,' Sonja nodded towards the young woman.

'Zdravo!' Sonja greeted the woman in her own language.

'Zdravo,' responded the woman, a little alarmed. 'How could you tell where I'm from?'

'That rosary around your neck, it's only worn by women from South America. But if it's not one of them, then, hun—got to be a Croat.'

'Nice to be recognised.'

'Not for me, they were making fun of me about my nationality.'

'Who?'

'These two,' Sonja pointed to Uhunoma.

'Which two?' asked the woman.

'This woman from Ghana here, and the woman from Nigeria, too.'

Uhunoma rebelled because she realised Sonja was implying she was Ghanaian: 'I am from Benin City, but no matter, my name is Uhunoma and you can call me Uhi,' she introduced herself in English.

'For me it is mattering who I am and what I am,' said the girl in broken English before she introduced herself. 'I am Ivona. Are you Christian?'

'Well, yes, I am,' answered Uhunoma.

'What do you know, a Catholic alliance!' Sonja switched to English.

'Not Catholic,' said Uhunoma softly, but the girl

and Sonja had already embarked on a more important conversation.

'Come on, if they insulted you, you don't have to go turn around right away and start insulting others,' said the young woman.

'I'm not insulting anybody, be whatever you like, but don't go waving that rosary around in front of me, damn it, all of you are just praying for the death of your enemies'.

'Should I be praying for your death?'

'Of course!'

The woman covered her ears with her hands and began to pray: 'Hail Mary, full of grace...'

'Fuck me,' Sonja blurted out. 'I don't need this!'

'Wait,' Uhunoma stopped Sonja who was about to head back to their corner of the yard, 'you can see she's still a kid, she doesn't understand anything, don't go writing her off so fast, after all she came over to us, remember?'

Sonja stopped, thought for a second, and then came back a few steps and pulled the woman's hands off her ears. 'What are you doing here, anyway? Why are you doing time?'

'Smuggling heroin.' The woman didn't blink.

'Alone or with your boyfriend?'

'Boyfriend, no way. With Zvonimir.'

'*Koji, brate, Zvonimir?*' Sonja switched to Serbo-Croatian without realising it.

'Hey, speak English' protested Uhunoma.

'Who the fuck is Zvonimir?' Sonja repeated the question in English.

'The head of the operation.'

'Where's he doing time?'

'He's off somewhere, in Croatia, Herzegovina, maybe on the Seychelles.'

'How come, didn't they arrest him?'

'They did, but I claimed full responsibility so in the end, he had a good lawyer, they released him.'

'Why are you telling me this now, aren't you scared of him?'

'He told me that when they release him I could say whatever I liked, because nobody would ever find him again, and besides Zvonimir isn't his real name.'

'This story reeks to high heaven,' said Sonja, while looking over at Uhunoma. 'I'd say Zvone was your pimp, and you went down for a handful of weed and now you're showing off for us here'.

'Doesn't matter, let's take her over to Nana,' said Uhunoma.

Nana looked Ivona over and was silent. Ivona suddenly planted her hands on her hips and pranced pompously around Nana in a broad circle, stopping a few times to spin in place and then on she went until she'd reached her starting point.

Nana clutched her head: 'Why do I need all this? Uhi, why did you bring me this little kitten?'

'Hey, girl,' she turned to Ivona, 'do you already have a mama here? Who strokes you and makes you purr?'

'Oh, no, she's not that stupid,' Sonja jumped in, 'the kid is treacherous, she eludes expectations, she's unpredictable, that's a quality, right?'

Sonja shot a questioning look at Nana and Uhunoma, but they didn't return their approval.

Nana patted Ivona on the shoulder: 'Unpredictability is the trait of a frightened animal,' and she turned slowly towards the prison building.

'What the fuck's up with the old lady?' Ivona asked Sonja. 'I thought she was a lesbian and I wanted to tease her a little.'

Sonja hugged Uhunoma and kissed her with the light touch of her lips, and then she answered Ivona: 'Free love rules here, but no teasing. Got it?'

Ivona clapped her hands over her ears again and started praying: 'Hail Mary, full of grace, blessed art thou among women...'

Uhunoma went back to her cell although the afternoon bell still hadn't rung. Nana was on her bunk, leafing through an old German magazine. The thought that she, too, could climb up on her bunk and turn her brain off by staring at pictures of the life of leisure of wealthy young girls made her stomach clench. Nana did that with such ease, while loathing everything; Uhunoma attributed this ease to Nana's life experience, but still she wondered whether it was possible that Nana had no desires. Even a little, strange, modest desire that would block her concentration, which would keep her up at night and steal her appetite at times.

.19.

Night. You lie there like all the other women in the tattered bedding. You look at the cloudy night sky, you clutch a random thing you picked up at the dining-hall the way children hug their cuddly toys—you need a bond with a world that is only yours, you want to imagine a friend, because you have none. You could fall in love with a pigeon, if only it were to fly to your window. The four walls of your cell are saying something, they are trying to converse with you, they want to teach you, they exert authority, but you don't give a fuck. The ceiling light goes out at nine o'clock; there are no switches in the cell. You can't see the bulb because it is covered by milky glass, but the glass is also protected by nothing more or less than a small mesh shield, firmly embedded in the ceiling. They are protecting the lamp from you. Probably so you wouldn't smash it, you wouldn't leave yourself lightless. And of course so you wouldn't cut yourself on the broken glass, assault someone else, inflict material or any other harm. You just would have played with the lamp. Used the switch to flick it on and off. Unscrewed and screwed in the bulb. And chatted with it now and then: the lamp is your third cellmate after all, it shares the good and the bad with you, it can tell you a lot about the cell's previous inhabitants, it can divulge a prison secret or two. But no, you mustn't hear those, it is in its little prison inside the prison.

Suddenly, it's as if the walls are pulsating, you have the impression that the cell is an internal organ in a vast body. The insides of the organ are close and stifling, they have no space for thinking, only for work, but what work is there to do? Work needs to be done in the brain, probably to engage the cerebral convolutions, they are the key to it all. Time to come up with one's own path out, it is simple, but nobody will give it to you. You have to discover it yourself, but first you have to pass through the wall, nothing easier! If you could pass through the wall—eh, here the big body already respects you, if you can, then choose the path you'll pursue further. So why the fuck waste time thinking? It is nothing but a pointless sifting through paltry experience, or, as Nana would say: a hand in a sack of rotten potatoes. Your mind needs to pass through the wall, pass through the wall, pass through the wall...

.20.

Uhunoma didn't dream, but half asleep she recalled the stories of an old man who helped her father plant vegetables on a family plot of land outside Benin City. For years he worked the soil for his neighbours because he didn't have his own plot. His father had left him nothing. The worst part of the job was the weeding. You could cut your hands badly, break out in a rash from the pollen on the weeds, any number of insects could sting you, but worst of all was if a poisonous snake bit you. Of course, there was a village healer, a wise man, call him what you like, who would lay leaves over the bite and, indeed, after a day and a half of fever you'd be as good as new. But sometimes that didn't work. Every fourth or fifth victim succumbed to the poison. Then the healer shrugged his shoulders, yelled at the boy whom he sent to bring the leaves, and—on we go.

That is why the old man, or so the story went, chose to trade night for day. He claimed everyone around him was in his dream, and he decided they were because he wanted to live and didn't want some mindless poisonous snake sending him to his grave. And they asked him, how do you know you're dreaming, how long have you already been dreaming, old man? He only laughed with glee and told them how he survived a bite by the worst of the poisonous snakes, the black cobra: 'I was clearing out a heap of dry brush that villagers had piled there for years by the edge of the village. I knew this was a place where there would be snakes, but, as usual, I knew I was dreaming and the snake's bite couldn't kill me. I tossed the brushwood from one pile to another so the boy who was helping me could pile them onto a wheelbarrow and dump them in another place. At one moment the pile I was throwing the brushwood onto grew taller than me. I turned to see whether the boy was on his way back with his barrow, when, at a level with my eyes, near the top of the pile of brushwood, only a metre away, I caught sight of a black cobra slithering among the dry branches. I didn't have time to react, I saw it fix me with its dead man's stare. It froze for a second and then spat its poison at my face. It's worst of all when poison sprays your mouth or eyes, there is no help for you, you fall to the ground like an epileptic and within a few minutes you're done for. But I knew what I had to do. Usually when you dream, something terrible is happening and you are desperately struggling to wake up, but you cannot, you seek proof that this is a dream, but to no avail. Actually, your dream convinces you this is reality and you, in the end, bow down to it—as I fell to the ground I uttered the time-tested formula: "Long live General Abacha!" I knew I never would have been able, awake, to utter these words and at that moment I woke up. Wonder of wonders: as a young man, in this same village, I slept on a friend's porch, my belly full, happy. I plumped the sack of yams under my head and dropped off back to sleep. That was the last time I woke.'

Everyone laughed at the old man's story, but they ruined his formula by informing him that Abacha had recently died: the dictator was poisoned by his teenage prostitutes from India. Rumour had it that one of them even sacrificed herself by pouring a large quantity of powerful toxin into her vagina immediately before intercourse, for Abacha didn't kiss any of them nor did he eat anything while he was with the prostitutes, in fact he never opened his mouth, he just fucked. The old man, father's assistant, swore at them later that they'd duped him, stripped him of his power of returning to reality. He is still sleeping on that porch thirty years ago, and who will wake him now?

.21.

'Hey, I heard there is an American woman here,' Nana jostled Uhunoma from sleep at an unknown hour of the overly long prison night.

'Probably more than one,' was all she, groggy with sleep, could say to Nana in hopes that Nana would give up on talking at the darkest hour of night.

'No, there aren't, Americans look after their own, when you stray from your home base. While you are in the United States, the watchword is "lie down and die, dogs", but as soon as you set foot on the soil of another country you become their ambassador of liberty, good will, and all the other American bullshit.'

'I have never met a bad American.' Uhunoma still hoped to fend off the pointless discussion.

'But who have you met? Who have you Nigerian women ever met in your life except your endlessly boring and foolish compatriots? And they're forever complaining: no money, no food, no cunt... But come on: at home you're all taken care of, and fat too, the fattest on the continent and all you do all day long is fuck. The best trick you pulled off was when you convinced the Europeans you're poverty stricken. Every appealing white boy and every cute white girl will fall for your "working-class" glamour and take you home. But you're the most ordinary lazy swine, you never wanted to work, in your country you acquire property by theft, and you chased us away because we were working honestly!'

Uhunoma was jarred awake by this barrage of insults, but even though they put her off, they also oddly pleased her. She wondered whether something could be both off-putting and pleasing, whether feelings like this arise from imprisonment, or if you never think about it but actually you're a walking perversion.

'Fine, we drove you out of Nigeria, so what do you want to say, what do Americans have to do with that?' Uhunoma joined the fray. Hats off, she said to herself, to whoever could remain immune to Nana's provocation.

'The Americans are cooking up an end for all of us. Do Afghanistan, Iraq, Somalia mean nothing to you...?'

'I know Somalia is in Africa, I remember that from my geography lessons. And I do remember that none of us children ever believed that Jerusalem really exists.'

'What do you mean, you pitiful child of Nigeria?'

'Like I said, we all went to church, we listened to the sermon, the pastor went on about the crucifixion and the resurrection, it was an interesting story about the faith that our grandparents adopted. But when we asked why they'd accepted this Jesus from the Mount of Olives, we were thinking that the mountain, and God's temple and the Pharisees, and all of Jerusalem, were somewhere up in heaven. Until my uncle ended up in Syria as a member of the United Nations forces. I remember that after he came back from serving in the army, he told the crowd of children who gathered on the street corner how he entered Jerusalem in the jeep. He thought he must have died because he saw a big sign at the entrance to the city that said: "Welcome to Jerusalem".'

'And what convinced him he was still alive?' Nana knew where the story had its twist.

'When a prostitute wanted to be paid.'

Both prisoners had almost fallen back to sleep, when Nana went on, 'But that American woman...'

'What about her?' said Uhunoma.

'She gets special treatment here. She was placed with the German and Polish women and they despise her because she is black with "privileges",' Nana explained.

'I don't believe she has any special privileges. It's her fault if she asked to be placed with German women. And why are American blacks so afraid of us Africans?'

'They aren't afraid of us, what they're afraid of is that if they are with us nobody will be able to tell them apart any more. I understand her, I had a white boyfriend, you haven't so you don't know what I'm on about.'

'How do you know I haven't?' Uhunoma grew bolder.

'Hey, girl, do you seriously think you can pull the wool over my eyes?' Nana cut off this thread of the discussion too and went off on a new tangent. 'The American comes over to me one day and asks me for a smoke. I tell her I don't smoke. Then she sticks to me like glue just the same and starts following me everywhere. First I think someone set her on me out of meanness, told her I was dealing, was the connection to the outside, hell if I know. But then I realise that she wants something from me, from me in particular.'

'And what is that?'

'Wait, don't interrupt me. She knew I was Ghanaian, she knew how long I've been in prison, she knew I have children. She knew everything.'

'So?'

'Don't you find that strange, my little rat?' Nana cooed. 'Where did she hear all that and why did she come over to me, don't you wonder, you're not interested? You think: an American arrives in prison and immediately knows everything about everything? Sure, they are the most progressive nation after all, why should I trouble my pretty little head about it?'

'I didn't say that,' Uhunoma protested.

'But you thought it. Listen, I saw fear in the eyes of that woman. You know, you look at that African face but in it you read a kind of fear, she thinks that all us Africans are cousins, that we'll sell her for a handful of rice, that we'll hang her from the nearest beam, strange.'

'But how did she end up here, I mean did she say what she's in for?' Uhunoma was beginning to take an interest in the American woman.

'It looks as if it has something to do with taxes. Evasion on a grand scale. I think she was up to something with the Americans on military bases here in Germany.'

'Well then why would she need you?'

'There you go, my clever little baby doll, your brain is working after all, don't you agree that it's odd how she knew all about my ex-boyfriend working with the army?' Nana pounded the underside of Uhunoma's bed triumphantly.

'Well fine, what did she want from you?' Uhunoma was searching for a clue.

'Ah, my dear woman, by Jesus and all the fat angels, she was just buying her freedom at any price. You really make me spell out everything: she told the prosecution she was prepared to squeal on any and all in return for a shorter sentence. They give her information about an inmate, and then she has to dig up something useful, something that will land someone else in prison or seal someone's deportation.'

'So what did you tell her?' asked Uhunoma.

'That I'd do the same thing were I in her place. But I have nothing to tell her.'

'Did she back off?'

'Of course. Show your pursuer respect and he will lose his will to pursue you. That's like when you start bugging your boyfriend for sex and he cools off quick.'

Uhunoma asked herself a random question before she fell asleep: 'So who is fucking the American?'

.22.

Father Ebermaier was sitting in his office, which also served as a modestly appointed chapel. At the back of the room there was a small altar with a wooden crucifix, on the wall to the right of the altar hung a reproduction of a Renaissance depiction of the Virgin Mary and baby Jesus. To the left was a peculiar, almost grotesque picture of an old man with a shaggy beard who was standing by the wall of a house in some city of Antiquity, his gaze angry yet a little lost. The man is leaning on a cane, and he is draped in a beautiful bright red robe. The lines of his face suggest he is old, but his thick hair and beard are still a deep brown, almost ruddy like his robe.

Ebermaier's desk stood under the tall window on the right-hand side of the room so that sitting at it he could always have the portrait of St. Nicholas he was so proud of in his line of sight. It had never been difficult for him to admit to himself that he was not a true believer, but this was why the thought of St. Nicholas, patron saint of travellers, the poor, and prisoners, was ever a consolation. To become a Catholic and believe in the saints struck him as apt, and all the Protestant claptrap about the purity of faith seemed more tailored to his inflexible father who never kissed his wife, their mother, in front of the children. The saints were of flesh and blood, proof that a sinful person could do good and be remembered for it. He'd never been carried away by the idea, like so many Catholic priests when they are young, that he might be called to the trials of sainthood. That was for someone else. He respected St. Nicholas as a friend, a man who understood and forgave him. Jesus had more important things to do than forgiving someone's petty vices and meting out penances: he was busy making a better world. And God? God was not interested in a better world; this was not a part of God's Magnum Opus. The little chapel reminded Ebermaier of his childhood bedroom which was always tidily whitewashed, no spiderwebs or dust, only a bed under the window and a shelf of books with religious children's literature. Now, instead of his bed, his heavy desk was beneath the window from which he sometimes gazed for hours at the portrait of St. Nicholas.

His thoughts were interrupted by a knock; into the room, or rather the chapel, came a young black woman.

She had straight hair, glasses with thin rims, she was of medium height, with slightly stronger shoulders, a narrow waist and ravishing hips, remarkable even under the shabby prison overalls: she was beautiful. While she stood at the door, waiting for permission to enter, Ebermaier openly looked her over, imagining every feature beneath the baggy clothes. Intentionally he left her standing there, he wanted her to feel a little uncomfortable, although he immediately concluded she was resolute. And she looked him over, which pleased Ebermaier. He knew that though he was well into middle-age, he was a good-looking man: he had a firm jaw, lips with a nice twist, not too thick, not too thin, and behind them his large, well-maintained teeth. A straight nose and big, brown eyes which had made him a real Lothario in his younger years. The figure he cut of an almost perfectly apportioned man was slightly marred by his thinning, very grey hair, but he had learned in time how to deal with it as if with the blessing of those who are wise and tested by time.

'Come in, child," Ebermaier grunted in a routine fashion in his serviceable English, enjoying the girl's approach. 'An encounter between a man and a woman is like a tumble through the stratosphere,' he thought. 'Do you know why I summoned you?' he asked the woman as if she had come to report to her superior officer.

The woman came closer and watched him demurely.

Ebermaier was almost a head taller and barely kept from succumbing to the demure gaze of the dark-skinned woman, thrown off guard a little, he said, 'You see, I know all about you so watch what you say to people. I am your polar opposite, whatever is said between these four walls remains a secret because I am the only person in this hotbed of sins who is incorruptible, unlike you, snitching and trampling everyone on your path.'

'You are not so incorruptible, Father,' said the woman, still with her demure gaze and expression, in a gentle tone, but not giving way. 'I know women you have paid to keep them from saying anything about their relations with you…'

'Logic is not your strong suit,' Ebermaier interrupted her and took a step back, but the feeling of insecurity immediately faded. 'You see, it's not incorruptible to be the person who buys off others, but to be the person who cannot, himself, be bought.'

'I have never heard this before,' laughed the woman and spun around and then took two or three steps towards the painting of St. Nicholas so the priest could see her bottom.

Ebermaier realised she was playing openly and he wasn't pleased that the woman had made the first move. 'Listen, child,' he tried to insert his already shaken authority into their repartee, 'your beauty means nothing here. Here you cannot find an honest husband, here you cannot raise children, here you cannot make friends. Your beauty here brings with it only trouble. I'm surprised you haven't learned this yet.'

'Thank you for your sincerity, Father, it is what is expected of you,' again she startled him with her answer. 'I like your attitude, and the way you slipped in that compliment. You are a true seducer.'

Ebermaier quickly lost his sense of excitement. He couldn't remember a single other prisoner who had irritated him this much, yet was so stunning. She would appraise him as if he were cattle at a country fair? This American loser, this Yank soldiers' whore who had learned her trade in the worst possible backwaters of Swabia and the Rhineland that only those American soldiers, especially those who weren't yet 21, thought were picturesque, romantic landscapes, and furthermore a chance for success in life. 'What a tragedy!' he thought, and he took a pack of cigarettes from his pocket, shook one partway out, drew it out with his teeth, and with his other hand flicked on the lighter, lit the cigarette and inhaled the smoke. 'A smoke?' he offered one amicably to the girl.

The woman took the cigarette and Ebermaier lit it for her.

'Sit down.' Now he was more courteous.

'Why, thank you,' answered the woman and sat on one of the several simple wooden chairs that were arranged in front of the altar. He perched on the edge of his desk.

'So this is the deal,' Ebermaier started, puffing smoke to the side, showing, by doing so, that he respected the person he was speaking with, 'a reporter from Munich was out to humiliate me at all costs by her scribblings. She kept coming to the prison and it felt to me as if she'd never give up until she found a detail she could use against me.'

'I value persistence,' said the girl.

'You are well equipped with cynicism, but that shell quickly cracks when the steel-toed prison boot stomps on you. And what is left for you then: nothing, a void, injured pride, the mad delirium of your own insignificance. No point in wasting words...'

'What do you want from me?' the woman was ahead of him yet again.

'Whoa, my filly, slow down! Your mind is racing forward, yet somehow you ended up here among us, meaning you must have been off in your judgement.'

'Perhaps... you are a pain, old man, why don't you go ahead and say why you summoned me, otherwise there is no point in wasting any more time here.'

Ebermaier couldn't find a way of launching into his speech from a satisfying position. What he wanted was to badger the girl, applying his routine strategy that gave the woman he was talking to no option but to do exactly what he said, and he always succeeded in this as long as he was able to maintain a tone that required penance.

'Tell me, child, where you spent more time in your short, young life. In the United States or Germany?' Ebermaier said with a conciliatory flourish.

'Good question, Reverend. I have never done the calculation. It must be that Germany and I are somewhere around fifty-fifty.'

'Then why don't you speak German?'

'I never went to school here. In fact I only went to primary school, and after that I jumped right into smuggling cigarettes and whisky.'

'Good lord, what a jewel!' Ebermaier blurted inadvertently.

'You will have to pay for what you're asking of me, you know,' said the girl.

'Of course, child, of course,' answered Ebermaier, pleased. 'So next time the Munich reporter shows up I have arranged for her to summon you. You'll tell her you don't know me.'

'That, at least, is easy.'

'Not so fast, my little dove, I have not finished yet. She heard, somehow, that there was a time when I helped dear Marta whom we all know and love, and now she is out to cook up a scandal over this.'

'Imagine that!'

'Don't mock me,' hissed Ebermaier. 'So, aside from

you saying you don't know a thing about any relationship between me and Marta, you'll also tell the pseudo-reporter that the main organiser for African female prostitution in Germany is right here in this prison.'

'Now that is something I have not heard.'

'Of course you haven't. I cooked it up this minute.'

'But why?'

'Oh good heavens, hear me out! You are lacking the patience gene, child, you're so totally short on focus. You'll give her the name of inmate Uhunoma Ahano as the mover and the shaker behind this entire African scheme. Do I need to write this down for you?'

'You said you cooked this up yourself.'

'What, you want it in writing? Do I sign off in blood? Come on, get serious, give that bitch of a reporter the name and we're good.'

'I will not.'

Ebermaier stood up from his desk, turned to the window and, without looking at the woman, snarled, 'What did you say?'

'I won't do a number on that girl. Find someone else.'

Ebermaier turned, lunged at the girl and thrust his face into hers. 'Why am I wasting my time on you? I have no time to interview all you little sluts, one by one, to find the one who is willing to say this most ordinary little white lie! What do you think this is, an audition?'

The girl jumped to her feet and headed for the door. Ebermaier blocked her way the moment before she could grab the door handle. With one movement he locked the door and slipped the key into his pocket. The girl planted her hands on her hips and with a sneer she looked Ebermaier in the eye: 'You old asshole, open the door, or you will regret the day you summoned me here.'

Ebermaier slapped her so hard that the girl staggered, fell over one of the chairs and then smashed her head on the altar. She struggled up onto her knees, sobbing, and ran her fingers over her lips. Blood dropped from a slash. She tried to stand, but then felt the priest's foot pressing down hard on her back. She tried to turn and fend off Ebermaier's attack, but then he grabbed her with one hand around the waist and ripped off her trousers with the other. She tried to scream but the priest's hand covered her mouth and she felt his penis pushing into her vagina. She was paralysed by the priest's force. In silence she sobbed and groaned, trying to pull in enough air, breathing frantically through her nose; Ebermaier had his hand pressed firmly over her mouth the whole time. He quickly climaxed, pulled out abruptly, shoved her down onto the floor, took the pack of cigarettes out from his pocket, threw one down to her, lit the other, and said: 'A cigarette after sex—just the job.'

.23.

For a few days, rain fell without stopping. The weather was gloomily overcast from morning to night, so noon felt like dusk. The stars weren't visible at night, and the grey of the clouds in early morning gave the day a strange solemnity and weight, as if beyond the clouds a serious judgement was coming, or a vast cleansing, incomprehensible to humankind. The walls of the prison became damp, mildewy, the time the inmates were allowed to spend outside, walking around the prison yard, was cancelled on the third day of rain, the inmates tracked so much mud into the building that it couldn't be cleaned by evening. For the first time since Uhunoma's arrival the governor addressed the inmates over the public address system. Nana translated the governor's articulate, slowly enunciated speech:

'Inmates of Bad Hallbach Prison, this is Steiner, your governor, speaking. Because of the heavy rains the decision has been made to stop allowing the afternoon exercise walk around the prison yard. Rain is forecast for the next few days, and after the precipitation ceases there will be no exercise sessions in the prison yard for at least two more days until the conditions for walking improve and the moisture levels fall. Let us work together for our mutual benefit.'

.24.

Ursula Heinz drove towards the prison and delighted in the first sunny day after the gloomy week during which she drenched her boots several times on her way to work and had to sit for the whole day in her office feeling as if her feet were sunk in sauerkraut. When she returned home and peeled off her socks, her toes looked like the toes of a wizened hundred-year-old woman.

Now she was driving down the motorway from Munich at 160 kilometres an hour, singing a familiar melody and soaking in the open sky that spread out before her, all the way to Bad Hallbach prison, and beyond.

She no longer argued with the prison guards, she greeted them all courteously; they, too, had made their peace and when she asked to visit Amanda Witherspoon and the prison staff did not object, she felt things were finally going to work out and soon she'd have the story everyone deserved to hear.

When Amanda came into the visiting area, Ursula was already sitting at a table, armed with a smile and a newly acquired persistence.

'You are Amanda?'

'Yes, that's me.'

'Thank you for responding to my request for a conversation.'

'You're welcome.'

'Some people I trust have recommended you as a trustworthy source.'

'Hmm, well, my thanks to them.'

'No, my thanks to you. I know you're having a hard time, and I know it's stupid to ask you at all about your own life, but there are a few things I do need to ask. Of course I will not be giving names in my article.'

'I understand.'

'How did you end up here as an American? Our readers think that in German prisons, along with our local criminals, there are only people from third-world countries.'

'Unfortunately, I ended up here because of the misdeeds of others. I completed my studies in the United States and came to Germany to pursue further education or a job. I arrived with my boyfriend of the time, who was a nuclear physicist.'

'A German?'

'No, an American.'

'He had a job at a German nuclear power plant?'

'Something along those lines.'

'How absolutely awful that you have to do time for something you didn't do. But I am here because of another story, one about Reverend Ebermaier.'

'I thought as much.'

'So you know that is why I contacted you?'

'No, I meant to say that I didn't think you'd come here for my story.'

'Oh, sorry, I'm sure your story is interesting, um, I mean, I'm sure it's powerful, but Ebermaier is the one who is a danger here for all of you.'

'Really?'

'Wait, have I said something wrong? I apologise again that I don't have time to hear your story. You know what, why don't you write it down for me, I'll give you my business card, here, you can take it, right, send me a letter, maybe I could work your story into the next issue.'

'That's fine, don't worry. Please, go ahead, what do you want to know about Ebermaier?'

'That bastard gave me a mouthful of foul abuse when I asked him about his intimate relations with women serving sentences here, and after that he started manipulating their statements, so I wasn't able to get anything from anyone.'

'Yes, he's awful, everyone hates him.'

'Did he behave that way towards you?'

'Of course, but it was nothing more than talk. He threatens everyone, but the stories about his relationships with the inmates are simply not true.'

'I received several letters from Marta Piatkowski, I believe you know her, in which she describes her relationship with Ebermaier in great detail.'

'Ha ha, everyone knows that Big Marta is a big fat liar!'

'What are you saying? The relationship didn't happen?'

'Why would Ebermaier pick that three-hundred pound beast for a lover? Don't you find that just a little odd?'

'Well, maybe you're right... Though what Marta wrote in her letters sounded so authentic.'

'Must be that Marta is an accomplished writer, perhaps you could hire her to write for the magazine!'

'You are so young and yet so bitter...'

'Life here teaches us that.'

'Can I believe you about Ebermaier?'

'Believe me if you like. Ask anyone you want. Who here even cares about Ebermaier any more? The fat, old, loony inmates are the only ones who even notice him any more.'

'Well thank you, Amanda, I almost took a wrong

turn... Perhaps it's best that I go, I need to think a little about the article.'

'Wait, who did you talk to so far about Ebermaier?'

'Why do you care?'

'I think I may have interesting information for you.'

'What information?'

'About a criminal who is here in prison.'

'What does this have to do with whom I spoke to about Ebermaier?'

'I think it does. Whom did you speak to?'

'A woman from Nigeria, let me check my notebook. Uhunoma Ahano.'

'I thought so.'

'What?'

'Uhunoma Ahano is a dangerous criminal'.

'How could she be, she is from Nigeria and doesn't even speak a word of German.'

'She runs a chain of illegal immigrant prostitutes in Bavaria.'

'That's impossible, she's barely over twenty.'

'Anything is possible with African women.'

'How do you know?'

'I have my sources.'

'Who are these sources?'

'Friends on the outside.'

'What did they tell you?'

'That she furnishes all the girls for the Frankfurt scene.'

'But prostitution is legal there.'

'Yes, but not if the prostitutes are trafficked illegal immigrants. Go to Frankfurt, check the identity of any of the African girls standing by the door to any of the porn cinemas on Moselstrasse and you'll see that they are not the people they claim to be and they hold fake documents.'

'How awful. All this is awful.'

'Uhunoma Ahano is still running the show right from here, from prison.'

'Are you a hundred percent sure of what you're claiming?'

'As sure as I am of day and night.'

.25.

Nana was sitting on her bunk, leafing through colourful scraps from her magazines. On the prison blanket next to her she had organised into several piles some clippings she had taken from a bag where she kept them all.

'What are you doing?' asked Uhunoma.

'I am playing meanings', answered Nana.

'What kind of a game is that?'

'So, see how I cut out shapes in different colours from all these boring German magazines? Germans deserve credit for the fact that their magazines are printed on top-quality paper, and the colours are so vivid that I'm ready to eat them, even when there are god-awful ugly dresses and tablecloths on the pictures.'

'You're cutting them out to make decorations?'

'No, silly! Come on, take a closer look,' said Nana mysteriously.

Uhunoma saw various geometric shapes that were mainly cut out of larger single-colour pages. The shapes were not all regular, some of them were reminiscent of clouds, ice cream cones, buses, fruit... Nana had obviously arranged them into some sort of order, but Uhunoma couldn't figure out what.

'Tell me... what is this about?'

Nana grinned conspiratorially. 'Why do you want to know? All this goes on inside my head, I don't believe you can understand how my mind works.'

Nana looked up and Uhunoma felt a surge of interest to know what this was about. She was swept by a feeling like the one when she was five and her older sister explained what it was her parents were doing behind closed doors when their father sobbed and mother screamed.

Nana stirred up all the clippings with her hand and quickly stuffed them back in the bag. 'Like this,' she said, lifting up the bag to Uhunoma, 'you dip your hand in and take out a clipping.' Uhunoma took out a round, orange piece of paper. 'There, so what does it remind you of?'

'I don't know, an egg, I guess,' answered Uhunoma.

'An egg, fine,' said Nana and laid the 'egg' on the bunk. 'Now reach in again.'

Uhunoma took out a green slip that appeared to have been cut from a photograph of the peel of an avocado, or maybe a cucumber, or maybe an apple. 'What now?' she asked Nana.

'Take a close look at the shape of the piece of paper and tell me what you see in it,' answered Nana.

Uhunoma looked at it for a bit, she even turned it over and saw printed text on the other side in German, with unfamiliar, long words. 'What am I supposed to say?' she asked.

'I can't tell you what you're supposed to say. Think hard, you must see something in that shape.' Nana wouldn't give up.

Uhunoma lay the clipping on her hand. She examined its edges, cut in the shape of little spikes. At that moment she gave an excited shout: 'Sun!'

'Good, good,' Nana reassured her with her teacher-like voice, 'now put the sun on the bed, too.'

Uhunoma placed the sun on the blanket and felt a strange playfulness come over her. She looked at the sun and egg and felt that the sun, the egg and she were in a far tighter connection than all the other things in the prison cell in any combination or in relation to her or Nana.

'Take another,' Nana encouraged her quietly.

Uhunoma took one more slip of paper and this time she recognised the shape immediately. 'Dog!' she exclaimed, almost inadvertently.

'Well fine, so be it,' confirmed Nana. And indeed,

the long shape of blue paper barely had any bulges, but now that Uhunoma had named it, it had to be admitted that the clipping could, indeed, represent even a dog.

'And now what do these three things mean for you?' asked Nana, hiding the bag behind her back because she didn't want Uhunoma pulling out any more slips of paper before she answered the question.

Uhunoma was excited, she wanted to say so many things at once: the sun for her was happiness, an attempt to make everything more beautiful; the egg took her straight back to her childhood, to a neighbour's yard where there were hens and the yard was always full of eggs, freshly laid and still warm. The children stole the eggs from the neighbour when he wasn't looking. And he was angry but not too angry. He knew the children would treat the eggs like treasure and when their mother came home from the market or from cleaning the homes of the wealthy, they would proudly display what they'd found and their mother definitely wouldn't ask where the eggs were from, that wasn't asked although everyone knew... And the dog? The dog ran around, barking at them while they were searching for the eggs—the boss's dog, what else could it do, it was protecting the hens and the eggs. But, like the boss, it had a soft spot for the children, it would nip at their bottoms when they reached for the eggs, but it never bit them; it barked, but never attacked. And it let them go home with their loot.

'You seem to be lost in thought, so that means you have figured out how to play,' said Nana.

Uhunoma swept up the three scraps of paper and offered them to Nana. Nana took them and stowed them in the bag that she set on the chair next to the bed. 'Feel free to use them whenever you like,' she told Uhunoma and jumped up. 'Time for lunch.'

.26.

Standing in line for their portions were Nana, Uhunoma, Sonja and Ivona. After Nana and Uhunoma were given theirs and went off to find a table in the dining-hall, Sonja shouted '*Nemoj ovde da me levatiš*' in Serbian to the woman, also from Serbia, who had been assigned to lunch duty and was dishing out the portions. The inmates turned to look at Sonja, but as hardly any of them understood that she was telling the Serbian server not to fuck with her, and the server didn't sound the alarm, their attention quickly returned to their daily routines. Sonja snatched her plate from the woman on the other side of the counter, with its generous serving, and then, to the surprise of the small number of people who were still paying attention, she handed that plate to Ivona and took Ivona's empty plate which she pushed in front of her with her usual gruffness. The server doled out the standard portion this time and then Ivona and Sonja joined Uhunoma and Nana at one of the tables.

'What was that about?' Nana asked.

'This kid is skin and bones,' answered Sonja indifferently, nodding in Ivona's direction.

'*Hvala ti*' Ivona thanked her softly in Croatian.

'Feel free, the two of you, to carry on in your language, but not here at this table. If you do have to go talking behind our backs, don't do it to our faces,' said Nana and winked at Uhunoma.

'Come on, old lady, chill. We're helping each other, that's how we survive, and you should be the one saying that, not me telling you,' said Sonja.

'I am not helping you, but if you think I'm helping, so be it: "let your enemy think you're his friend." I remember a complete wanker who used come by to visit us at home in Accra and he was always quoting the Koran. So there, that is what I say to you, believe whatever you like, and me—leave me alone.'

Unaccustomed to Nana's sermons, Ivona responded in her broken English. 'Sonja wanted to say we all need to give each other a hand. *Ruka ruku mije*.' At that Sonja and Ivona burst out laughing.

'What are they laughing about?' Uhunoma asked Nana.

'God only knows,' answered Nana and patted Uhunoma on the shoulder.

Sonja explained, 'Ivona said, "one hand washes the other and money washes them both".'

They all enjoyed their meal.

After lunch, Uhunoma went to what they called the lounge, a medium-sized room where the prisoners watched television. A sports channel was on, showing a broadcast of track and field events. The starter had just fired his pistol and eight women wearing different coloured jerseys sprinted off in a race. After ten seconds the first to cross the finish line was from Jamaica. A dispute erupted among the Germans in the first row. They argued fiercely and Uhunoma noticed Marta joining the fray. They were quarrelling about who had won, when the camera showed the disappointed German racer who sat down on the track and plunged her head between her knees. Marta stood up abruptly and immediately knocked over two or three unoccupied chairs around her. Uhunoma watched her move away from her countrywomen, to whom she tossed something in passing without turning. Marta came straight over to her and extended a hand. The German women from the first row began laughing aloud. Then Marta spoke to them in her poor English: 'I make no difference about the colour of the skin. All people are same.'

'*Du bist ein MTV und Jenki Fanatik. Dummkopf!*' jibed one of the German women.

Uhunoma responded to Marta with her hand extended and Marta clasped it, pumped it vigorously the way politicians do when having their picture taken at an international meeting, and then pulled her to get her to stand up, still not releasing her hand. Uhunoma realised that Marta wanted to take her along so she pretended she knew what this was about. She followed Marta out of the lounge and down the corridor to Marta's cell. When they reached her lair, Marta tried to explain to Uhunoma what all the secrecy was about: 'You were lucky. A girl cancelled her place on the shopping trip. Tomorrow you go in her place.'

'I have no money, how can I go shopping?' Uhunoma was perplexed.

'No, no, no!' Marta began slapping her forehead again, 'You will call Nigeria!'

'How?'

'I will be with you and I give coin to you so you call... *aus der Telefonzelle.*'

Uhunoma felt a surge of joy and wanted to hug Marta, but held back. 'Oh, thank you, thank you!' She clapped her hands together the way Catholics pray and brought them to her chin, she wanted Marta to understand how grateful she was.

'So tell me, *Ebermaier ist zu dir gekommen*? Ebermaier, priest?' Marta was clearly upset. Uhunoma had heard something about the relationship between Ebermaier and Marta, but she didn't want gossip to spoil her opportunity to call home.

'I don't know anything about the priest. He doesn't interest me.'

'*Lüg mich nicht an!*' Marta fumed. 'You know Ebermaier! Ebermaier came to you! Bitch!'

Uhunoma realised Marta's feelings were hurt. She touched Marta's shoulder and asked her gently, 'What did I do wrong to you?'

Marta flopped back onto a big pillow at the head of her bed, moving the bed against the wall, so hard that Uhunoma felt the vibration of the blow under her feet.

'*Idiot! Ih hasse ihn!* I hate him,' Marta uttered the words in English in a slightly more friendly tone. 'He doesn't come to me any more. Now he likes... the thin ones more,' Marta gesticulated, placing her palms one next to each other, leaving a very small space between.

'I know he something... wants to you... ' Uhunoma gleaned that Marta was warning her of a possible danger that Ebermaier might pose for her, but she didn't know what she could do about it.

'Don't worry, you tomorrow to go with me out, call Nigeria.'

Uhunoma thanked her again and went out the open door of Marta's cell. She wasn't worried about danger that might be lurking because tomorrow she'd finally be hearing the voices of her loved ones. Ever since they caught her and took her to the first prison, she often wondered whether her family was thinking about her as often as she thought about them. The first paper shapes she cut out of Nana's magazines she dedicated to her family: a green rectangle represented her childhood home, a violet square for the role of her school, and a yellow circle for her mother.

Back in her cell, after closing the door, Uhunoma asked Nana while she was cutting out shapes, 'How did you get the scissors?'

'Every day, even now, after lunch I leave my dessert untouched for the prison cleaner.'

.27.

The opacity of night was once again coming on. It should be easier to breathe at night, but instead it is worse. The air isn't fresher, it is denser. As if nocturnal darkness has a thickness to it, as if it has physical substance, it can be measured out, weighed: you breathe in and it enters your lungs, but also your ears, eyes, it enters you all over... it rapes you. Damned night rapes you in the nastiest way, it never pounces; instead it waits for day to retreat and then in it comes, always slowly, no rush. Like a drunken local big man to whom girls are brought, sure that he is their only chance for success, success that treats them like some common object bought from a store. It is night that brings all this together.

In early evening Nana complained to Uhunoma of a dizzy spell. She was quieter than usual, moaned a little in bed, and then dropped off to sleep. Uhunoma hated the nights when she couldn't fall asleep quickly. The night pressed down on her, and morning was kilometers away. A person who has never suffered from insomnia cannot imagine how long a night can last. Longer than an entire day, longer than a week, month, year... And especially when you cannot leave your room, when you cannot even turn on the light. Some girls do push-ups, their muscles bulge, they do ab crunches, they're ready for a fight at breakfast because energy like that needs an outlet. Sometimes she wished she could cry, because crying soothes, drains, but she couldn't. There was little left inside her that could move her to tears.

And you get tough. Hard as stone, as a rock, as dried bread, as a shank of beef. To soften it you need to grind it, soak it, cook it.

'Uhi, Uhi...' Uhunoma heard from the lower bunk. She leaned over and saw Nana, her prison pyjamas unbuttoned, gasping for air. Uhunoma jumped down and helped Nana sit up. Nana whispered for her to call the doctor. Uhunoma began banging the cell door. Officers soon came and took Nana to the hospital wing. Nana limped and coughed. She didn't even turn around before they shut the cell door in front of Uhunoma.

Why had they taken Nana away? Would they bring her back? What was wrong? Why hadn't the doctor taken better care of her? Uhunoma did not want to stay alone, she did not want to be alone in the cell. It wasn't even midnight yet and there she was, alone. She froze there by the cell door and tried to still her own breathing; she kept hoping to hear voices from the depth of the corridor, the on-duty nurse would probably give Nana a pill and send her back to the cell. But no voices. The whole prison was asleep. Uhunoma suddenly felt as if they'd all left. She knew this was a silly thought. Where would they have gone: no one would get out, no one could get out, neither the prisoners nor the officers. But that entirely unfounded feeling of fear of being alone in the entire building, in the whole world, really, overwhelmed her and she didn't know how to deal with it or how to keep it at bay. She stared at Nana's empty, rumpled bedding and the longer she stared at it, the more she was overwhelmed by panic. She went over to Nana's bed and ran her hand over the sheets as if to convince herself that Nana really had been lying there only moments before, that Nana wasn't merely a figment of a dream of hers. Now all the dark, nocturnal forces would conspire against her, they'd attack her with all the weapons they had, she had to quickly pull herself together and ready her defence. There they are, they're coming... she felt their march in her ear drums, their triumphant chant, they are coming to celebrate your defeat.

Uhunoma sat on the floor, stared at the wall in front of her, and resolved to await the demons of the past with her eyes open wide.

The first to appear was her uncle, who'd died after she'd arrived in Europe. He was wearing the same shirt he had on the day when she began to hate him. He often pinched her bottom when she was a little girl, or with one hand he'd grab both her little hands, while with his other he'd grope for her breasts that were only just starting to bud. She already knew what he was after, and she also knew she didn't yet have what he wanted. Her older sister, however, who was only two years older, already had everything that drove her uncle wild, everything that turned this otherwise mild-mannered minibus driver into an unbridled lecher. It was December and a powerful harmattan wind had been blowing for several days, piling up layers of choking Saharan dust. One such windy evening he came to her and her sister in their bedroom. He and his wife looked after them while her parents were in the village, sowing the seasonal vegetables that fed the whole family. As soon as he came into the room he grabbed Uhunoma's sister around the waist and told Uhunoma to lock the door. Uhunoma wanted to run away but her uncle stopped her and ordered her to stay. She locked the door and without a word she watched her uncle roughly tear off her sister's clothing and rape her in silence. Her sister Eniye tried to defend herself but she did not cry out. She would have brought shame upon herself if she had woken the other members of the household and that would have been worse than the pain she suffered in the brief minutes of their uncle's assault.

Her uncle then faded from view and before her on the wall of the cell appeared the female customs official at the Murtala Muhammed Airport. The slender, tall woman in a uniform and with a military cap over her thick, straightened hair lectured Uhunoma when she was about to board a plane for Europe using counterfeit documents. The woman locked her in an interview room and ordered her to strip naked. Then she gave naked Uhunoma a speech on the state of the country and the network linking international elites to the criminal forces in Nigeria. She raged on about Nigerian traitors and colonial degenerates who do not love their homeland. She told Uhunoma that she knew the passport was fake and that she was off to Europe to become a cheap prostitute. She told her she'd call in a whole detachment of customs officials who'd line up to take their turn with her, and then she'd send her to prison where the guards would do the same. She thrust her face at Uhunoma, took her by the chin, and with her big, beautiful, penetrating eyes she searched for signs of fear. 'Do you have any morals at all?'—the customs official's question echoed in Uhunoma's ears. The torture was interrupted by the group leader who was taking the girls illegally from Nigeria to Turkey. He pounded on the door and demanded that the official open up. Hesitating at first, she opened the door, and the group leader, a man in his early 30s, slipped her a twenty-dollar bill. The official suddenly became an altogether different person: she quickly picked up Uhunoma's clothes off the floor and handed them to her, saying: 'Come along, child, get dressed, you'll miss your flight.'

The image of the customs official faded on the cell wall and instead there appeared the image of a Turkish businessman in his expensive Italian suit. For weeks after she arrived in Turkey, Uhunoma was sure she was already in Europe. Izmir looked like the beautiful cities on European post cards, and the startled and sometimes creepy looks from Turkish men didn't alarm her too much. Only after a few days before the 'boss' arrived in the flat where ten of the Nigerian women were staying with the three 'group leaders'—two of them Nigerian and one from Senegal, one of the other women informed her that they were in Asia, not Europe. The 'boss' was a Turkish businessman who owned seaside properties on the Aegean and whose wife was a corpulent Nigerian woman. She persuaded him to run a sideline, smuggling people into Europe. They could bring them into Turkey with no difficulty, but then they had to get them through the Balkans, using their Turkish and Nigerian connections in the West, and into the European Union. Uhunoma caught the eye of the Turk as soon as he first came to the flat in Izmir to see who had come with the newest round of immigrants. The next day he came to the flat and asked her to go with him. Uhunoma knew what that meant; she had no choice but to do as he said. He wasn't ugly, in fact he was decent looking. He took her to an average Turkish restaurant where they had a good meal, and then in his expensive car he drove her round the city and took her to one of his empty flats. There was no furniture in the flat but a large mattress on the floor, and right next to it, a small refrigerator in which the businessman kept expensive wines. They shared a bottle of red wine and then made love. This was the first time she'd slept with a white man and saw that there was nothing different between them and blacks. Both of them fell asleep as soon as they climaxed. Then she quickly dressed, slipped on her shoes and started for the door. At that moment she felt the 'boss' grab her by the ankle. 'Where are you off to, my little dove?' he said in fluent English, smiling. Uhunoma didn't hesitate but snatched the empty wine bottle up off the floor and waved it at him. 'Don't, please!' the businessman managed to get out, but Uhunoma smashed the bottle over his head a moment later. He lay there, unconscious, covered in broken glass, with a thin stream of blood dripping down his forehead. She left the flat, and decided she wouldn't go back to her group. She spent three years knocking about Izmir and other Turkish cities, was in brief relationships with

Turks, Italians, Syrians, Greeks, until one of them, again using counterfeit documents, brought her to Portugal. There she found her first job. She worked as a cleaner and dishwasher in a soup kitchen, again with counterfeit documents, of course. After a year she heard that a friend of hers from Benin City was living in Lyon, married to a Frenchman. Uhunoma moved there and moved in with them, but the Frenchman wasn't happy. He kept complaining to his wife that Uhunoma wasn't doing anything, that the state would confiscate their apartment if they were discovered hiding an illegal immigrant, and they wouldn't be able to have children while she was living with them in their small flat. Uhunoma packed up her things one morning and left for Germany...

The image of the German policeman who had asked for her identification papers and arrested her faded from the cell wall with the first rays of morning light. The door of the cell opened and Uhunoma, after the night she'd spent, was no longer sure whether this was a demon or a prison officer coming into the room. The demon or prison officer ushered in a young black woman who was carrying a small bundle and clean sheets. The door slammed shut, and the new resident spoke to Uhunoma, who was sitting on the floor, in a recognizably American accent: 'Bitch, make my bed!' and threw her sheets in Uhunoma's face. Uhunoma pulled them off and moved to stand up, but Amanda kicked her hard in the chest. Uhunoma fell onto her back on the floor and Amanda went over to her and squashed Uhunoma's hand with her shoe.

'Why?' sobbed Uhunoma.

'Keep your mouth shut and do as I say! Clear?' shouted Amanda.

Uhunoma grabbed Amanda's foot with her free hand and yanked it hard, so Amanda lost her balance and staggered back a few steps. Uhunoma stood up quickly and ran at Amanda with all her strength. She managed to grab her by the hair and smash her head on the side of the upper bunk, but Amanda rebounded with surprising speed and from her crouched position she punched Uhunoma two or three times under the ribs. Uhunoma dropped to her knees and fought back against the pain, but then came the deciding blow of the knee to Uhunoma's jaw that threw her back all the way to the toilet. Although Amanda had stopped attacking, Uhunoma retreated to behind the toilet and fingered her numb jaw to see if all her teeth were accounted for.

'Do something like that again and you'll be dead meat,' said Amanda. Then she lay down on Nana's bed. Soon she was snoring while Uhunoma wept quietly behind the toilet.

.28.

At lunch, Sonja and Ivona looked for Uhunoma and Nana. They'd almost finished eating when they caught sight of Uhunoma, taking her portion and going to a table to sit alone. Sonja nodded to Ivona and together they both went over to Uhunoma.

'Uhi, what's wrong?' A glance at her swollen face told Sonja that Uhunoma hadn't slept the night before.

'Nana is in hospital.' Uhunoma could barely speak.

'What happened?' Sonja took Uhunoma's hand, but Uhunoma didn't respond, she didn't even look up.

'*Nisam znala da su toliko vezane*,' said Ivona in Croatian, 'I had no idea they were so close.'

Uhunoma shot her a scornful glance, stood up and turned to go back to the counter, her lunch untouched. Sonja also rose and went after her. There was an unusual kerfuffle going on at the counter. A woman from Romania was arguing heatedly in a garble of English, German and Romanian with a dishwasher from Ukraine. A group of tall, muscular Ukrainian woman had already surrounded the Romanian woman and she could no longer reach the counter, where prison rules dictated she ought to leave the tray with her dirty dishes.

The Romanian woman turned to the surrounding Ukrainians and yelled: *'Bagamias pula in fata ta!'* Then she headbutted one of the Ukrainian women in the belly, knocking her to the floor. The rest of the Ukrainians dragged her away from their friend, threw her to the floor and began kicking her savagely. At that point the Serbian woman doling out the food leaped over the counter with a huge frying pan in her hand and shouted: *'Strömt ab!'* From behind she whacked the head of the largest Ukrainian among the five or six who had surrounded the Romanian. The largest immediately dropped to the floor, the first next to her turned and received an identical blow from the front, and then she, too, was out of commission. The rest of the Ukrainians shrank back, while the Romanian woman lay, cringing, on the floor. The onlookers split into two camps: those who supported the Romanian and Serbian women and those who sided with the Ukrainians.

When the fight erupted, Uhunoma and Sonja found themselves among the Ukrainians, while Ivona was left in the crowd cheering for the Romanian woman. The incident had gone on for little over a minute when a detachment of officers charged into the dining-hall, batons swinging, and beat everyone who didn't instantly obey their order *'Neider!'* Sonja, tall as she was, held Uhunoma by the shoulder, but at the same time she had an overview of the situation in the hall and immediately realised that an oblivious Ivona was going to be bashed on the head by a baton. So while some of them ran towards the hall door and others crouched behind the counter, she ordered Uhunoma to lie face-down on the floor, and then in several bounds she reached Ivona and pulled her down under a table. Within three minutes the officers had imposed order, and after this the nurses came into the dining-hall and, with the officers' protection, escorted the prisoners to hospital.

Uhunoma took her place in line on the corridor, along with all the other prisoners who had been in the dining-hall when the fight broke out. After ten minutes of standing and staring at a point in front of her, while the prison officers ran up and down, pulling a few Ukrainians and Romanians off for questioning, Uhunoma regained her composure and for the first time she began thinking about everything that had happened since Nana had been taken ill the night before. First, she didn't know whether Nana was still alive. This thought upset her and her eyes filled with tears. Then she remembered

Amanda, and she was suddenly afraid of going back to the cell. And then the worst thought of all hit her: the fight had ruined her chances of going to the supermarket with Marta that afternoon, so her long-awaited call to Nigeria was yet again beyond her reach. She felt bereft of hope. There was no fight left in her. All she cared about was hearing that Nana was okay, that and nothing else. 'If Nana is doing well, everything else will be fine.' When she caught herself hoping for a positive future outcome she scolded herself, wriggled her toes to feel there was still the thrum of life in her, and fended off any impulse to hope for anticipation.

A little farther down the corridor from Uhunoma, Sonja and Ivona were standing next to each other. Nobody dared turn, say a word, even look left or right, if that had even been possible without moving the neck muscles. Still, Sonja very slowly moved her left hand, pressed to her side, and lightly brushed the fingers of Ivona's right hand. At first Ivona's fingers did not respond, but after Sonja's hand lingered for several long moments in one place, Ivona's did move—her little finger and ring finger slowly, imperceptibly, clasped a small part of Sonja's hand.

'To your cells,' rumbled the deep voice of one of the female officers. The line of women became a column and marched down the corridor, and though nothing special could be read from Ivona's and Sonja's facial expressions, a blaze had ignited inside them that even the most capable fire brigades from the world's largest cities could not have quelled.

.29.

Uhunoma milled along the corridor with dozens of the other inmates. They were being led to their cells, she knew that, but the walk seemed long and aimless, as if they'd never get there. And when they did get there, what would she do? There was no point in staying in this Bavarian prison. Until now there seemed to be a point, an atonement of sorts, a kind of cleansing, but now the slog had lost its meaning. Not because she was afraid she wouldn't be able to get through it, but because she knew she could. Yet why, for whom? Just like Nana said, this isn't any sort of penance, nobody is watching over you and nobody is trying to improve you, it's just that you have fallen into a ditch and you can't climb out. All you can do is trudge forward along the muddy, smelly bottom of that ditch. If you want to play dice with fate, you can turn and go back, or keep on moving ahead. To keep moving ahead is so predictable and so inevitable that sometimes it even seems ridiculous. Going backwards is also funny, literally, walking backwards, but it's tiring, too. To walk backwards provides amusement for the leisurely, but there is no place for it when blows are raining down on all sides.

Uhunoma marched through the streets of Lagos as part of a vast funeral procession. This was no ordinary funeral—never was there one like it ever before or since. In fact she wasn't in a proper procession; the streets of the city were teeming with people who were all moving in the same direction: towards the home of singer and activist Fela Kuti. Fela had died of AIDS and all of Nigeria knew this was a major battle that had been irrevocably lost. When the Kennedys and Martin Luther King were killed in earlier years, the most vulnerable in Africa and in the rest of the world took their deaths as a call to arms. But Fela's death spurred no one to fight, only to a celebratory dance, for nobody felt as powerful as he had been, and nobody aspired to be like him.

Uhunoma had come to Lagos to visit her aunt, but the next day the terrible news spread from mouth to mouth all the way to her aunt's modest home in Ikeja. Word had it that a funeral would be held in ten days time in front of Fela's house. That tenth day in the morning it seemed as if absolutely everyone had come out of their homes; this river of people was embarking on a new exodus. Never before had Uhunoma seen such festivities: both young and old, women, men, even tiny children, all danced and moved slowly towards their destination. Deep basses and the blaring sounds of saxophones and trumpets emanated from a truck on which Fela's band played for a full seven hours—moving along the ten-kilometre route from the morgue to Fela's house. Uhunoma only knew that Fela was a hero. She thought of him as a wild preacher, almost without sex or age, who could send anyone into a trance. The words of his songs reached every person because he poured into them the street rage of the poor labourer, as well as his famous phrases and favourite interjections, which were always, without exception, cutting and genuine. But, coming as she did from her quiet, modest life in Benin City, she had thought of Lagos as a city of bounty and prosperity, and now when she found herself there for the first time, she had to face up to the fact that Lagos was much poorer than her native city, probably poorer than all the Nigerian cities put together. And Fela lived here, in Ikeja, surrounded by all the poverty and suffering he sang about. Although she was only a fifteen-year-old in whom seethed every imaginable, contradictory feeling, she, too, was caught up by what was happening and joined in the dance and festivities, celebrating the demise of an idea.

With Uhunoma was Festos, her sixteen-year-old cousin who, at home, had whined and whinged like a little brat, but as soon as he was left alone with her he turned into her knight in shining armour, his chest swelled, he put on a sleeveless tank top to show off his thin but firm muscles and truly gave her a sense of safety. The two of them watched the river of people pouring in from all the streets and byways, dressed for a party, which for the poorer men meant white shirts, and for the women, brightly coloured dresses, but there were many who didn't even have festive clothes, so they danced, shouted, clapped, men and women alike, wearing nothing but a sleeveless tank top, like the one Festos wore. Uhunoma held his hand because though the mood was entirely peaceful, she was anxious and frightened at the size of the incredible crowd that kept growing and growing.

'This scares them,' said Festos, bouncing a little to the rhythm the crowd was moving to.

'What?' asked Uhunoma.

'These people,' he said, waving at the multitude around them and then, in passing, patted a little boy on the back of the head.

'But who are "they"?' She couldn't figure out why someone would be afraid of this happy, dancing throng.

'The ones who have everything,' he shot as if from a gun.

At that moment Fela's band, parked nearby, struck up the opening chords of the song *Everything Scatter*, and it was as if the crowd had been waiting for this. They all stopped and began to shake and twist as if they were burning with fever, or, worse yet, were possessed by evil spirits; some laughed, others had a painful grimace on their face, as if experiencing real suffering. The three-minute intro to the song built up expectations. And then Fela's entire group exploded, and Uhunoma realised that she was changing. With every last person in the crowd, she knew what was coming after those first three minutes—she knew the melody by heart just as everyone else did, and suddenly she felt she no longer had to hold Festos by the hand. She could fling her arms in the air or drop her arms to the ground, and once the moment came and the melody exploded—nothing would be ever be the same. Fela had given the street his energy and it would always be here, that much was clear, she felt this as did everyone. As if she had been carrying this knowledge, only a few seconds old, inside her since forever. And truly, from that moment on she knew what the world was made of: fury, suffering, hatred, faith. Never again would she be able to turn her back on reality.

The song erupted and everyone started yelling, running up and down as much as the jam-packed streets allowed, leaping and spinning around. Uhunoma could no longer see her cousin. She gave in to the throng and for the next half hour, while the band was still on the same song, she danced and had a glorious time and felt as if this dance was the most important fact in her life and that the doors of another dimension had opened, the dimension the toothless village healers had always told her about, a dimension that was always present and to which you can always return, the one that makes you free.

When the music paused for a moment, cries of 'water, fresh water' echoed through the streets instead of bass and saxophone. Children were selling plastic sachets of water that everyone needed after a half-hour of dancing in the sun. Where had these children come from, where were they filling the sachets they carried—suspended in clusters from a hoe—over their shoulders? The water couldn't be too far away. Some people were offering water from their front doors, but each time one did, a hundred people would crowd around them and only the nimblest got their hands on the free water. As she had no change on her, she decided to follow a skinny little boy who had sold all his sachets; with the hoe in one hand and a pile of bills in the other he quickly pushed his way through to a side street. She knew he was going off to fetch more sachets so she set out after him. This wasn't easy because the boy bent forward and wriggled between people who were still shouting, flinging wide their arms, dancing. At one moment the crowd began to

move and just when the boy slipped into a little alleyway
a few metres from her, the crowd drew her with them
in their own direction and once she'd finally scrambled
out at the street corner, the boy had vanished. Still, she
made her way down the alleyway on a gentle downward
slope, giving her the strange sense of moving against
the current: she let herself slip among all the arms, legs,
heads, bellies, bottoms of the sweaty and euphoric people
who were following the sound of the music and eulogies
and who with their movement upward were pressing
her among them in the opposite direction, downhill.
Then someone from below shouted: 'Police!' and the
crowd began jostling and everyone tried, over the person
standing nearest to them, to elbow their way through to
the top of the street. This stopped Uhunoma's advance
against the current and she leaned back against the wall
of a house to avoid the crowd until they all forgot that
dangerous word that someone may have shouted just
for the hell of it, or under the influence of the powerful
cannabis that always circulated at Fela's concerts, and, of
course, at this final one.

Her move did not turn out as she'd hoped—the
crowd began pressing her more forcefully against the
wall. She grabbed hold of iron bars that supported a
sort of improvised balcony, partway up the building the
crowd was crushing her against, and with the strength
of her upper arms she lifted her whole body out of

the heaving multitude like a gymnast, while pressing off the wall with her feet. Then slowly, first with one hand and then with the other she grabbed the railing on the balcony and hoisted herself a little higher, until she finally managed to work a foot up onto the balcony deck. The view from up on the balcony was astonishing: beneath her, only a half metre below, a river of people was coursing by and all were pushing and shoving and trying to break through towards the end of the street to find a little space and join the head of the procession as quickly as they could, hoping to reach Fela's house before entering it became impossible. She stood on the balcony, alone on those two square metres, and felt as if she were afloat and had unexpectedly been entrusted with a privileged position she didn't know how best to use. The balcony door opened and a girl, maybe a year older than she was, smiled and invited her in. Had it been any other situation, Uhunoma would never have accepted the invitation, but now she felt as if she couldn't go wrong, and besides, how had she found herself up on that balcony if not by letting her gut feelings guide her?

She entered the room, darkened by heavy curtains, as was the custom in Nigerian homes that couldn't afford air conditioning. On a well-worn sofa a man with grey hair was sitting next to a grey-haired woman, both dressed in stunning brightly coloured traditional attire.

'Good day, young lady,' said the man in a raspy,

soothing voice. The woman next to him nodded, and the girl who had brought her into the room invited her to take a seat on an armchair, also well-worn, facing the sofa. Then the girl went into another room and brought back a pitcher of water and several glasses. The man stood, poured the water into a glass and offered it to Uhunoma. She thanked him and drank it down to the last drop.

'Today is a big day,' said the man, 'we're glad you have joined us. An unexpected guest is a blessing on every festive occasion. Let me introduce to you my wives: Adio and Olufema, and I am Tobi. Where have you come from, young lady? You are not from Lagos, this much we can see.' Tobi smiled. 'My name means "God is good" although one might not say this was the case when looking around. Let me guess. Are you from Benin? It has been a long time since I have seen such neatly arranged tribal scars.'

'I am, Sir.' At that time Uhunoma was still addressing every person older than herself as 'Sir' and 'Madam'.

'I am glad you are here and I won't ask how it occurred to you to climb up onto our balcony', said Tobi in an amused tone, eliciting a smile from Uhunoma.

Tobi's older wife, Adio, said, 'You are brave, little girl. Do you know anything about Fela, and who he was?'

'No, I do not', answered Uhunoma sincerely.

'Adio used to live in Kalakuta. She can tell you all about him', said Tobi.

Adio got up from the sofa and took off the kerchief that had covered most of her naturally thick, short-cut, curly hair. She was very beautiful, a narrow face and large, slightly slanted eyes. Uhunoma thought she might be over fifty, but Adio was one of those women who become more beautiful with age. As Fela's band had struck up one of their better-known tunes, Adio began ever so slightly to dance. She swayed her hips and moved her hands as if in conversation with an invisible friend. While slowly dancing she began her story:

'After attending schools in Britain and beginning to play Afrobeat in the United States he decided to come back to Nigeria and remain here regardless of the peril for him'.

Uhunoma looked over at Tobi and Olufema. They began dancing with their hands to the rhythm of the muffled music that came from outside and dictated the tempo of the story Adio was telling. The whole room filled with a pungent odour, and Uhunoma realised what was going on when she saw that Tobi had taken a spliff from his pocket and lit it. Thick whitish smoke spread around him, and the heavy, familiar smell wafted in her direction.

'He came back and founded Kalakuta and the Afrika Shrine where we all converged and danced from morning till dark. Kalakuta was a commune that provided free medical care for all who sought it and was a haven for everyone fleeing the military authorities. Fela proclaimed Kalakuta to be a republic and whenever the government was upset with him and threw him in prison, the people came out onto the streets, as they have today, and demanded his release. Because of this the government never dared to have him killed, and they wanted to, they longed to every time he spat in their faces. Lagos became the centre of the free world thanks to Fela, in the middle of an enslaved Nigeria that was still being ruled by colonial flunkies, thieves, freeloaders and murderers. For everyone he was an example of how to ignore your fear of the powerful on the one hand, and how to outfox them with cunning on the other. How to educate yourself when nobody provides you with an education'.

Olufema took the spliff from Tobi, inhaled two or three hits, then handed it to Uhunoma. Uhunoma had never smoked marijuana before, nor did she ever do so again. She couldn't remember anything about how she sucked in the smoke, but somehow she must have because she remembered the way the ceiling became the floor and the floor the ceiling and the horror she experienced, listening to the rest of the story. Each word Adio uttered sounded as if it came from somewhere deep inside, from inside her own head, from her own lungs... Uhunoma felt herself losing consciousness.

The politicians and their rabid dogs despised Fela. They were constantly outraged by his licentious lifestyle. Although they themselves had no morals to speak of, the measure of things for them was their own hypocrisy with which they laid the new foundations for what they called independent Nigeria. This is why they were appalled by Fela's candour and his lack of concern for order. Fela had no need of air-conditioning, tiled bathrooms, luxury cars or lavish receptions, everything that all politicians dreamed of and what was for them their sole goal in life. On the streets of Lagos they stood eye to eye with Fela who spurned all this and every day he was prepared to risk everything to preserve his consistency, and he displayed this through his loyalty to the poor. So they locked him up every few months, beat him up in prison and tortured him, but he told them he was made of rubber and they couldn't do anything to him. Every time he came back from prison his large family in Kalakuta greeted him raucously, and he would display his fresh wounds and, bristling, he'd roar 'They cannot touch me!' Within a few years he had changed from being a promising young man to becoming the protector of the city until the day when the army marched into Kalakuta and razed it. On that day, twenty years ago, hundreds of soldiers, armed to the teeth, charged into Fela's house and first they assaulted the women. They tied up all the men and beat them, including Fela, with their rifle butts.

They took the ill from the free infirmary and heaved them out the window, along with Fela's mother and brother. His mother died of blows to the head. Then they bound the women's hands and raped them en masse. They raped the fifty women they found there, and this lasted for several hours. Meanwhile they beat the men between the sessions of rape. Then they kicked them all outdoors, like mangy dogs, and set Kalakuta ablaze. Fela lay, insensate, on the road.

Adio moistened Uhunoma's lips, brought her back to consciousness, and helped her clamber up off the floor and onto the sofa.

'You knew Fela?' asked Uhunoma.

'After Kalakuta was destroyed, he organised his wedding to twenty-seven women who had been left with no roof over their heads. I was one of the twenty-seven. Although there wasn't a day he didn't sleep with a woman, I never slept with him, not before the wedding, in Kalakuta, or afterwards. He claimed he married us to protect us and give us a roof over our heads, in keeping with Yoruba marriage traditions. He would have slept with me, as well, if I hadn't been related to his cousins from Abeokuta! For many of Fela's performances Tobi played the drums in Lagos in the 1980s and the moment came when I chose to move in with him. We've been living together ever since. Olufema joined us last year because I could never give Tobi a child. Now we are blessed,' and she pointed to Olufema's swelling belly. 'We are not attending the funeral, I cannot stand seeing it. I cannot bear the thought that the big men in the senate and government are now overjoyed. Off you go, little one, it's worth seeing Fela, even if you only see him lying in state. Never again will you have the opportunity to lay eyes upon such a man.'

Adio continued swaying to the rhythm of the fading music, and Olufema took Uhunoma out to the street, which by then was passable: most of the procession had moved on a few blocks to the north. She walked through streets that widened and narrowed, and the music from the truck throbbed in her temples; she imagined that cockroaches and gigantic mosquitoes, the regular inhabitants of the infamous Nigerian prisons, were laying their eggs in Fela's open wounds while he lay, groggy from beatings, in the urine of the other prisoners. For in Nigerian prison there are no toilets, no beds, no chairs, no blankets. You piss where you lie.

Uhunoma staggered over to a ditch by the side of the road and vomited into it. When she lifted her head, much weakened, there was a little girl standing there, wearing only shorts, and in her reedy little voice she called out: 'Fresh water, fresh water!'

.30.

Uhunoma walked into the cell and found Amanda sitting on the bunk, her fingers laced behind her head. She seemed relaxed but closely watched Uhunoma's movements.

'Apologies for this morning,' Amanda said, breaking the silence, 'I should have beaten you up so much more.' Uhunoma stepped back from the bunk bed, she didn't know whether to expect a new assault. 'Ha, ha, come on, don't be afraid, I'm too tired to beat you now. Come, have a seat!'

Uhunoma didn't care to sit on what had been Nana's bed only the night before, next to this violent brat, at least five or six years younger than she was, who belted a punch as if she'd been boxing since the age of nine. But what other option did she have? She sat cautiously on the edge of the bed, in such a way that, Amanda, if she wanted to hit Uhunoma, would have had to lean forward and that would have given Uhunoma enough time to get out of the way.

'Do you think they'll organise the trip to the supermarket next week again after cancelling it now?' she asked anxiously, trying to keep her unease from showing in the colour of her voice.

Amanda looked at her as if she'd just announced that she wanted to sleep with a turtle, or eat soap for breakfast. 'Of course they won't.' She sat up on the bed before Uhunoma had a chance to react and jump to her feet, and then she put her arm around Uhunoma's shoulder and through a scornful giggle she declared the holy truth. 'The trips to the supermarket are every other Thursday in the month, full stop. My little African warrior, didn't you see the prison schedule? Can you read? You'll have to wait till next month, but who knows whether you'll even be on the list then.'

Uhunoma's voice failed her. She meant to say something, to stand up to Amanda, but she was limp. Her desire to have someone feel compassion for her won out. If this was to be Amanda, then so be it.

'When will the time come for me to take that trip? Will I ever make it to that pay phone?'

'You won't,' Amanda said, her pupils widening with the satisfaction of breaking this news to her.

In the half-dark of the cell and the shadow of

evening, Amanda looked like an unreal creature from a man's carnal dream. The whites of her eyes shone beautiful, her young face seemed to delight in its own features, and her pink hands moved around on her body, as if communicating and playing an external game of seducing the person she was talking with, in this case, Uhunoma. Might this be unintentional? Or was her confidence in her own beauty yet another assertion of superiority?

Uhunoma once more bit back her pride and tried to start again from the beginning. 'Can you please help me make a phone call?'

For the first ten seconds Amanda gave a full-throated laugh. Then she came right up to Uhunoma's face and looked at her from only inches away. Uhunoma felt her warm and sweet, slightly moist breath but didn't flinch. Amanda looked her over, stared into her eyes, lips, nose, as if she were examining a cheap, pretty dress to see whether it was really just a 'second'. Uhunoma also studied Amanda's face, her smooth skin—free of tribal scars—youthful and feral. Amanda was still a child who was game for a fight, out to prove herself, unschooled and belligerent. Uhunoma let slip a little smile, because she was thinking about what Nana would have done to Amanda if the two of them had been cellmates.

'What are you grinning about, little miss airhead? All of you bitches are circumcised. You fuck with no feeling. I'd kill myself. Tell me, what is life like with no clitoris? What does it feel like? Wait, wait, don't tell me, I know, it's as if you're a man, just—with no dick!'

This didn't hurt Uhunoma much. Amanda was right and it wasn't a hard call to make. Almost all the girls from Benin City whose parents had come from the villages to live in the city had been circumcised. For centuries this had been their tradition. Uhunoma enjoyed sex, but would it have been better if she hadn't been circumcised? She couldn't say. Women her age weren't doing this to their daughters and this was already an answer to the question of what was better. Inside herself she wished Amanda were circumcised. God willing she'd succumb to the razor of some blind old aunt!

'Why do you need a phone booth anyway? Don't all of you in Nigeria wield special powers? Don't all of you practice voodoo, aren't you all fucking witches?' Amanda was on a roll. 'What do you need a phone for, when all you need for communication is to link up through your thoughts, what is that called? Telepathy! And you talk with the people there in Africa, for free!'

Amanda was having a grand old time, while Uhunoma was finding the conversation more and more interesting. The cocky American didn't know how to stop.

'A minute over the phone is so much more worthwhile for me than all the telepathies of the world, to hear the voices of people I love, so I know they are alive,' Uhunoma said, more to herself.

'What's that?' asked Amanda.

'Nothing, I was wondering who invented the telephone,' Uhunoma answered only to avoid any further conversation with Amanda.

'Not Nigerians, that's for sure!' hissed Amanda maliciously.

.31.

The day after the fight, the prison governor ordered everyone to spend the whole day locked up in their cells. That day was long for all the women in the prison. The governor didn't often meddle in prison routine; he signed the decisions about staffing new male and female officers, the schedule for who was going on vacation when, the invoices for supplies, the prison menus, the reception and release of prisoners. Few of the inmates had ever seen him. There was no conversation with the governor nor were there speeches from him to the prison population. The women in the prison knew the governor only as the 'voice' that was occasionally broadcast over the public address system with announcements in German regarding the functioning of the penitentiary as a whole. The 'voice' was always cold, a little sad; he sounded like a teacher close to retirement and for most of the women at the prison this gave them a feeling of melancholy, though nobody blamed him personally. Nothing was different this time either, while he read the decision on the disciplinary measure of full-day detention in cells that applied to all prisoners, regardless of who had taken part in the fight and who had not.

Sonja spent that day doing push-ups and crunches while her sluggish cellmate, Elena the Russian, nibbled chocolates she had received in a package from the outside. Sonja awaited the next morning calmly. As soon as the door opened she stepped slowly into the corridor. Ivona's cell was only fifteen metres or so from hers. She reached the door, slightly ajar, and pushed it lightly. Ivona was asleep on the upper bunk, and on the lower bunk sat a girl who was laying cards out in a strange order.

'*Ciao*,' Sonja greeted them softly in Serbian.

'*Dobar den*,' said the girl in Macedonian. The conversation between the two proceeded in an undefined mixture of the languages of ex-Yugoslavia.

'What are you doing?' asked Sonja, curious.

'Looking into the future,' answered the girl.

'And, what do you see?'

'Nothing much,' said the girl.

'So I thought,' concluded Sonja and stood up.

On the upper bunk, Ivona's face was resting on her pillow, her eyes closed. Her black eyebrows twitched slightly every few seconds.

'Do you know her?' asked the girl from below.

'Yes, I believe I do.'

'Watch out, she's a wild child, sometimes she wakes up in the middle of the night and shouts, babbles nonsense, then she's back asleep in seconds. I ask her what's going on and she doesn't answer and, just when I think she's fallen asleep again, she starts shouting and howling. Now I'm used to it, but if they move her to another cell, man, I'm telling you, she'll have trouble.'

Sonja stroked Ivona's hair and Ivona opened her eyes. Her lips moved into a little smile. Sonja answered with a smile. She leaned on Ivona's bed and came right up to her face. Ivona kissed her suddenly, like a child who runs to their parent to plant a kiss on them out of the sheer joy of it. Sonja then gave Ivona deeper, more serious kisses. Ivona hugged Sonja and began in a frenzy to shower her cheeks, chin, ears, hair with kisses. All tall and lithe, Sonja took hold of Ivona, who was much smaller in build, lifted her up from the bed and set her down in front of her on the floor. Ivona took a step back, and Sonja leaned over and kissed her gently again. Ivona turned a little anxiously towards the Macedonian woman who was still sitting on the lower bunk, laying out her cards.

'Didn't see a thing,' said the Macedonian without looking up, 'but hold your horses with the public displays of affection in the hallways. You'll get into big trouble. Kid, you're best off pretending to be a slave to this Claudia Schiffer of yours, walk behind her, head bowed, don't speak before she speaks, because otherwise the little old ladies here will catch on and you'll become consumer goods.'

'Hey, I'm no lezzo!' Ivona shouted at the Macedonian, while still holding Sonja's hand.

'Of course you aren't,' said Sonja, pulling her in and kissing her. The kiss lasted for a half or even a whole minute, and then they both smoothed their hair, tucked in their shirts, and left the cell, Sonja first, Ivona after her.

'Best of luck,' said the Macedonian.

Nobody can be sure they'll serve out their prison sentence without a hitch, even if they swear they'll obey the officers, steer clear of trouble, and sincerely repent their sins. Prison is not that sort of institution. It is not a workplace to which you come to do your part and in return receive a salary and respect, make friends and ultimately take on a mortgage so you can buy a flat. It is not an association one joins out of conviction, nor a political party joined by people who share your views, it is not even an asylum for the homeless, for lepers. Prison cannot be compared with any other institution, and as to how long prisons have been around, only church is equally venerable. Prison stands, in a way, at the junction where all roads meet. No matter whether you are on your way to work, or a robbery, or a farmer's market, or a holiday, you may end up in prison. The well-fed never trust the hungry. Someone who is infirm cannot imagine how healthy people are able to walk the world or how little chance there is to do so. And so it is that prisoners don't believe in the existence of those who are at liberty. Of course a person in prison longs for liberty at every moment, but the fact that a higher power, the power of the law, has locked them up in a narrow cell with one window or sometimes no window at all, gives them the feeling that nobody anywhere is free. Each person who is free may say: 'Prisoners find this thought a comforting one,' but if anyone who is at liberty ends up in prison they quickly change their tune.

Sonja walked down the corridor and Ivona followed along behind her. They didn't comment on what the Macedonian had recommended, but instead simply internalized her words. Now every alliance and every helping hand meant more than defiance and playing the hero. If they had stood outdoors by the fence and kissed, as they longed to do, first they'd be pulled apart by the officers, as public displays of affection were not allowed unless you found yourself in a quiet corner, a place where you couldn't be seen by those who shouldn't see you. But far graver consequences came from the other prisoners: the jealous ones who would do whatever it took to make the couple miserable, the more hysterical among them blaming the couple for all their problems, the evil ones—blackmailing them.

'Ciao, ladies,' Cristina, an Italian inmate, greeted them, 'the elderly woman from Ghana who sits with you at lunch had a heart attack the night before last.'

'No way! Nana?' asked Sonja, alarmed.

'Eh, yes, that's the one, Nana. Apparently the old woman barely pulled through, she is hooked up to life support, but she's on the mend. They took her to hospital. If they hadn't she would have died.'

Sonja had a look at the Italian woman. There was no reason for her to invent something like that. Cristina was in her late thirties, her thick dark-red hair spilled loose around a bandanna, she was loud, and always smiling. She always knew everything about everything that was going on in the prison, she knew most of the inmates by name, and with all problems of a practical nature that were a constant torment for inmates she did whatever she could to come up with a work-around, offered herself as spokesperson to the prison administration: nobody had ever appointed her to this position, nor was anyone else interested in doing the same, and the role suited her perfectly. With time the inmates began coming to her as well with their personal problems, to talk through their cases, the details from their trials, the appeals proceedings. Cristina always listened closely and with surprising ease she also remembered the details, so she had the reputation of serving as the prison 'defence lawyer'. She preferred to speak of herself as a 'union rep', and the Germans called her a communist. Someone from the ground floor spread the rumour that Cristina was an anarchist terrorist who had been captured in Germany. So there were Germans who called her 'Raf' after an old woman prisoner from the RAF, Rote Armee Fraktion, who had been serving her sentence at Bad Hallbach until a few years earlier.

'When will she be allowed to come back?' asked Sonja.

'When she recovers,' said Cristina.

Sonja looked over at Ivona, seeking sympathy in her eyes and then felt a pang of concern: did Ivona feel nothing for Nana? Maybe she didn't care. This was entirely possible and Sonja wouldn't have been able to her forgive her. This would dramatically quell her passion, the joy she felt that she'd found someone with whom she could share the grim and bleak days of their pallid existence.

But before she had the chance to read anything in Ivona's eyes, she felt someone clasp her hand and squeeze her fingers. The hand was Ivona's, consoling her, invisibly, while her face remained perfectly cold. Ivona watched Sonja out of the corner of her eye, as if her hand was giving the words of consolation without restraint—words had nothing to do with the cool head and reasoning of this young Croatian woman from Herzegovina who'd been sacrificed by a petty criminal on one of his trips to the West.

Sonja turned, slipped her hand out of Ivona's and strode quickly towards the dining-hall toilet. Ivona followed her. Sonja looked around to see if anyone was watching, and then quickly went into one of the stalls, pulling Ivona in after her. Ivona grabbed Sonja's breasts and squeezed them.

'Hey, that hurts,' Sonja protested while pulling off her shirt.

'Try mine,' answered Ivona and she, too, pulled off her shirt.

In the cramped stall, where there was hardly any room to move, Sonja and Ivona stood, bare to the waist, hugging. Sonja's breasts were small with budding nipples, while Ivona's were large for her petite build, her nipples small and round. Ivona kissed Sonja's stomach where her muscles were clearly defined: Sonja's torso looked like the body of athletes who strut around on the track before a race begins. Then Ivona started unfastening Sonja's trousers, which quickly dropped to Sonja's knees and her hips were now covered only by underpants that were two sizes too big.

'The supplies manager gave them to me,' Sonja said.

'Fuck the supplies manager,' laughed Ivona and put her hand on Sonja's bottom, poised to slip down her panties. Sonja took her hand and gently steered it away. Then she slipped her other hand into Ivona's jogging pants and tucked her fingers into Ivona's underwear. With her finger she stroked Ivona's warmth and pressed into it. Ivona began jouncing up and down and moaning softly. With the hand she'd just used to keep Ivona from pulling down her baggy panties, Sonja covered Ivona's mouth so nobody would hear what was going on in the stall. It didn't take long, Ivona squirmed faster and faster against Sonja's finger, and after a few convulsive thrusts of the pelvis she groaned like a wounded dog and bit Sonja's fingers. Sonja bit her lip to hold back a sob. Ivona nearly slumped to the floor, Sonja could barely keep her from falling; as if her body had changed, it had gone heavy and limp. Sonja told her to pull on her shirt and tie her hair back in a pony tail, and she also rearranged herself. She gestured that Ivona should be the first to leave, which she did and quickly closed the stall door behind her. Sonja leaned on the wooden partition in the stall and waited long enough that nobody would connect their going in together with their exit from the toilet. She waited and inhaled Ivona's fragrance which filled the little stall and reminded her of lilies of the valley.

.32.

The cell was quiet. Amanda snored. Uhunoma could not sleep peacefully. The day the inmates were locked in their cells had been twenty-four hours of torment. Amanda introduced rule by terror, and Uhunoma did not have the resilience to stand up to her. She decided she would not get out of bed the whole day. Like a malicious child, Amanda had decided that no matter what it took she would prove that Uhunoma was totally in her power. Uhunoma naively encouraged this, like every patient victim, and hoped her persecutor would give up. Amanda also stayed in bed all day, but whenever Uhunoma fidgeted on the top bunk Amanda threatened to punch her. Uhunoma tried not to move for hours, and whenever she did move inadvertently, Amanda would jump to her feet in a fury and punch her. Uhunoma wept without a single audible sob, and her body went rigid. The next morning, when Amanda went out into the corridor to stretch her legs, Uhunoma could barely clamber down from the bed to the floor and moaned with the pains she'd suffered from keeping all the muscles in her body tense and immobile.

'Uhunoma Ahano!' came the voice over the public address system. She hurried to get dressed as fast as possible, but before she'd managed to get dressed, two officers arrived to escort her out of her cell. They noticed that Uhunoma was in so much pain that she couldn't bend her legs to put on her trousers so they helped her, but without an ounce of compassion. They weren't rough with her, they were merely following orders. Rough treatment may come with a frisson, with emotion. Even if the feelings are twisted and scary, they are human. You believe you change them, that you can flip the frown into a smile. A person who is carrying out an order with no compassion has no capacity to do anything of their own free will, their concept is limited to the length of time it takes to do a task. If the officers were rough with Uhunoma, her body would hurt more, and at one moment she'd refuse to collaborate and they'd need twice as much time to force her to dress. If they were to feel compassion for her and try to help her dress—that, too, would take too long, because the woman suffers the blows and cannot be compelled to do anything speedily in that condition. Therefore nobody feels anything, we are all just doing our job, 'And I, too, am doing my job,' thought Uhunoma.

This time the officers did not take her to the meeting room, but to one of the offices in the administrative wing of the building. Despite the pain she suffered while she walked, she brightened as soon as she entered the area designed for the daily lives of people who were free.

The staccato of a person typing, a relaxed conversation among office mates who aren't worried about whether someone is listening to them or not. And phone conversations... How wonderful to listen to an ordinary phone conversation of an official you don't know, words heard through the door of a neighbouring room, ajar. Everyone doing something, managing tasks that had nothing to do with her, functioning like all office workers, and there she sat in the hallway on a chair upholstered in artificial leather, not even wearing handcuffs—because they hadn't left the prison grounds. This could be a town hall, a post office, a registrar's office, or any other place like that. The officers buying themselves coffee from a vending machine, not even looking at her, after all there was no way to escape. Through a window? She'd find herself still in the prison yard with a towering wall between her and freedom. 'Doing my job!' Uhunoma said again to herself.

They waited like that in the hallway for almost half an hour, until two men who were oddly different—one tall and fat, the other short and skinny—emerged from one of the offices, and without a glance at Uhunoma entered the room she was sitting near. The officers then gestured for her to rise and they escorted her in.

The men behaved as if this was harder for them than it was for Uhunoma. Both were dressed in decent suits with ties. They couldn't decide whether to sit at the large office table in the middle of the room or to stand, so they spent several minutes debating in German about who would sit and who would stand. In the end they indicated to Uhunoma that she should sit on the chair facing the table, and the skinny man said, 'We don't speak English so good. Understand everything, but speaking... not so good.' He shook his head. 'We wait for translator.'

'Why?' asked Uhunoma.

'I said you, we speak English bad,' repeated the skinny man.

'I understand,' answered Uhunoma, 'but why did you summon me?'

'Against you a serious accusation,' said the fat man.

Uhunoma thought maybe Amanda accused her of starting the fight in the dining-hall. 'That fight was not my fault!' she protested.

'Fight? What fight? In Frankfurt you hanky panky illegal immigrants!' the fat man picked up the baton.

'I have never been to Frankfurt, what are you talking about?'

'Aquasex Theatre, Frankfurt, twenty immigrants arrested, fake papers. You go-between,' the fat man pointed his meaty finger at Uhunoma.

'We haves proofs,' said the skinny man.

At that moment a young man with long hair tied back in a ponytail entered the room, his face wearing a slightly puzzled look. He greeted them in German and introduced himself. This was the translator and he was explaining—now Uhunoma understood—to the policemen why he was late.

'Hello, I am Halid,' said the man with a slight Slavic accent and extended his hand to Uhunoma.

The police warned him in German that fraternising with prisoners was not allowed. The man withdrew his hand, but still gave Uhunoma a friendly smile.

The skinny man launched into the story and the translator translated: 'On the night of 25 September of this year at the aforementioned locale in Frankfurt we discovered that the aforementioned Aquasex nightclub had unlawfully hired nineteen persons who have not regulated their status in the Federal Republic of Germany. Moreover, for several of them there is reason to suspect that the club owner had unlawfully deprived them of their freedom.'

Uhunoma tried to connect Frankfurt and this nightclub to her stay in Europe. The last time she'd been at a nightclub was in Turkey, but since she'd arrived in

Europe she had only been in clubs and cafés when she was there as a cleaner, working half-time for a temp agency at a club run by an Arab in Lyon.

'You are suspect to organise to bring to Germany these people,' the skinny man said in his clumsy English, 'and here you continue with crimes.'

'I have never been in Frankfurt, soon after I came to Germany the police arrested me and ever since then they have been moving me from one jail to another.' Uhunoma realised that this misunderstanding might cost her years of her life and she broke out in a cold sweat.

The fat man slapped his open palm on the table and, his voice growing shriller, he said, 'You have no proofs that you are only coming into Germany then.' Then he signalled to the translator to translate what he'd said, in case Uhunoma hadn't understood. The translator leaned over to Uhunoma and quickly said, 'You know, you have the right to a lawyer.'

The fat man instantly clutched the translator by the shirt, slammed him back down into the chair and screamed at him in German. The translator tried to justify himself by saying, in English, 'I am just respecting the law!'

'Well fuck your mother you moron!' cursed the fat man in English.

The skinny and the fat policeman withdrew into the

corner of the room to consult about what to do next. The translator gestured subtly to Uhunoma that she shouldn't say anything. Uhunoma understood what the translator wanted to tell her and when the policemen returned to the table she responded *Ich weiss nicht* to all their questions, this being one of the few German sentences she had learned. The police were furious with the translator, but after they'd given up on any further examination, they still quickly told him what he should convey to Uhunoma. He translated for her: 'You will be charged with violating federal immigration laws, with criminal association for the purpose of depriving persons of liberty, as well as with collusion in planning and realising international organised crime.' Uhunoma didn't know whether she was supposed to say something or not. She decided, finally, not to speak, as the translator had urged.

The skinny man decided to address Uhunoma directly: 'Who your collaborators? If you give us their names, the court will reduce your sentence.'

The translator said nothing and stared at the floor. Uhunoma knew the police were asking her to give them a name. That was all they cared about—to be given the name of a person they could go on harassing, and so on and so forth. And who would arrest the man in Turkey and his wife who were bringing in girls as models, receptionists or babysitters and then turning them into prostitutes? Would anyone believe her if she gave his name as a co-conspirator? Perhaps. But he was outside their jurisdiction.

The policemen exchanged glances, swept their files up off the table and said goodbye with a sarcastic *Aufwiedersehen*. The translator followed them out, with a quick 'Good luck' to Uhunoma.

.33.

Uhunoma decided that, no matter what, she would find a way to make peace with Amanda. But this was not easy. How can an underdog call for a ceasefire? Nobody asks them. However if the underdog has allies there might be some way to gain ground, to strategise. After Amanda spent a full two days beating her up in the cell, Uhunoma pulled herself together and began thinking about how to stop Amanda's savage behaviour. She understood that Amanda was not the only source of her troubles. But she needed peace with Amanda so she could bring back her awareness of where she was and what her chances were of extricating herself from this nightmare. That is when she remembered Ebermaier. He was the only person who could offer her some degree of protection, she thought.

One morning, after Amanda had settled fully into life in their cell, imposed her order and reduced

Uhunoma's territory to only the upper bunk, Uhunoma said, 'I like Ebermaier.' She decided to take the risk and float Ebermaier to Amanda as her protector. She wasn't expecting much, but there was a chance that pretending acquaintance with Ebermaier, who was known to everyone as a womaniser, she might build the beginning of her defence against Amanda.

Amanda's eyes opened wide, but it was clear that this was no longer the rage and fury she had been venting. This was more fear, as if the very mention of Ebermaier alarmed her, as if the mention of his name could serve as some sort of serum against her aggression, though Uhunoma didn't know why.

Amanda said, 'I swear I'll kill you, so help me God!'

This sounded half-hearted to Uhunoma, and, in comparison to the overpowering terror of the last few days, the sentiment sounded more like a call for help. She sensed that now was the moment to fight for herself. She slowly turned towards Amanda, completely ready to put her in her place. The fear in Amanda's eyes spurred her on. She grabbed her by the arm and shoved her up against the wall, and with her feet she trapped Amanda's feet. Amanda swung her head and bashed Uhunoma in her forehead which sent her head spinning, but she did not let Amanda go. Two or three times she slammed Amanda's back against the wall. Amanda tried to use her feet to kick Uhunoma away, so Uhunoma slapped her twice, hard, and Amanda slumped to the floor. This was the chance Uhunoma had been waiting for. She began kicking Amanda in the back, chest, head. Amanda had no chance to scramble up before Uhunoma had picked up the only wooden chair in the cell and brandished it.

'I'll kill you,' shouted Uhunoma, holding the chair over Amanda's body.

'Don't!' pleaded Amanda.

Uhunoma stopped, suddenly a hush reigned in the cell, the only thing she could hear was her own rapid breathing. She put the chair down and watched Amanda, who, panting on the cell floor while blood dripped from her mouth, lost all the superiority that had, until a few minutes before, guaranteed her inviolability. Amanda rose very slowly, but then, abruptly, as if shot from a cannon, she hurled herself at Uhunoma, punching and kicking and chased her into a corner of the cell. Uhunoma, however, hadn't released her grip on the chair. With one hand she pulled it behind her as she slunk back, and with the other arm she fended off the blows. Then she pushed off from the wall, gripped the chair with both hands and shoved it straight into Amanda's face. The chair cracked right across Amanda's nose, and Uhunoma got in a swing and bashed Amanda with it in the chest. Amanda instinctively shielded her body with her hands, but Uhunoma smashed her on the back and hip until the chair broke into pieces. Then she grabbed Amanda by the hair and dragged her over to the toilet. Amanda fought back, but Uhunoma managed to push her head into the toilet bowl and flushed. Then she punched her another three or four times in the kidneys and let her go. She took a few steps back until she reached the broken chair, broke off one of the legs and again, now with the slab of wood in her hand, returned to Amanda who was moaning by the toilet. They eyed each other for a time. Uhunoma didn't hit her any more.

'You African asshole, you think you have it hard?' Amanda groaned hoarsely through weird laughter interspersed with gasping sobs. 'Know why Ebermaier doesn't fuck African women? He's scared shitless of AIDS! That's your salvation, you poor kid, if there were no AIDS, Ebermaier would have claimed you straight away.'

Uhunoma eyed wounded Amanda who was no longer a threat to her. 'How do you know these things about Ebermaier?' For the first time Uhunoma was asking Amanda a question without having thought long and hard about it first.

'Because he... raped me.' Amanda started to cry.

'I'm sorry,' said Uhunoma though she didn't know if she really was.

'Don't give me that shit, you don't give a fuck,' wailed Amanda.

'Not true, maybe Ebermaier fucked you, but I'll be

fucked over by the German police, they want to stitch me up with these prostitutes in Frankfurt.'

Amanda stopped crying and brushed away her tears. 'I'm the one who stitched you up.'

'What?' Uhunoma had never thought someone in Europe would mess with her fate to that degree. What gives you a sense of security, as an African woman, on this continent is that most of the people can't tell you apart from any other black person, man or woman. This is a hopeless yet sometimes reassuring feeling, one that Europeans know nothing about, when nobody counts on you, when you are surplus, beyond the reach of statistics and annual plans, utterly outside the equation. And now, all of a sudden, here was someone writing an equation just for you, why this was practically an honour!

'That lady reporter from Munich began taking a look at Ebermaier and he was scared she'd get to you before he did.'

'How would he get to me?' Uhunoma still didn't fully trust Amanda. 'Nana, my cellmate, told me all about him the first time he showed up in our cell.'

Amanda scrambled up from the floor, stripped off her bloodstained shirt and dried her hair with it. 'I promise he wasn't after your pretty eyes, he was interested in coercing you. But now the Bavarian police have you on their list of leaders of organised crime and getting off that list is very, very difficult.'

Uhunoma's throat tightened. Where was her liberty now? She felt she couldn't breathe. She wanted to get out of there, out of this hell, she couldn't take this any more. 'I want to go home,' she sighed, resigned.

'Too late. They're in need of fresh blood. Someone to blame, to lock up for ten years, to serve as an example. They don't care if nobody learns a lesson from this, all they want is to flex their muscles. You Africans end up getting shit on because you're uneducated, you don't have lawyers to help you, a lobby, wealthy sheiks, Chinese multi-billionaires. You are the workhorses. And we need workhorses. You don't know much about this. In the States we have Mexicans who work for us, the Japanese have the Koreans, and so on...'

'And you, like, you understand everything going on all over the world?' Uhunoma still detested Amanda.

'Of course, is that so very difficult? Tell me, what is it you don't get? You don't see that Ebermaier is out to get you? You don't get it that you're in prison only because you don't have the proper papers? You don't get it that I have stitched you up with ten years of prison just because you're a fucking Nigerian? Ah yes, you didn't ask me how I dragged you in.' Amanda sat on the bed, she pulled a moist tissue from under her pillow and went about cleaning up the cuts that were starting to swell.

'So you told the police everything?'

'That's not how it works. I wasn't the problem for Ebermaier, the reporter was. Ebermaier blackmailed me:

either I'd snitch on you to the reporter or he'd tell the police about my dealings with American soldiers. What would you have done in my place?'

'Wait a minute, you asked Nana that too!' remembered Uhunoma.

'So?'

'Nana told me that you snitch on others so you can reduce your sentence. I think I trust her more than I trust you.'

'Look, everyone hates me, they all want to fuck me, the officers, the prisoners, the German women, the Poles, the Turks, the Moroccans. And now, what am I playing at? Why the fuck should I be principled when in exchange for my principles I get a kick in the ass? Come on, come on, you would all be just like me if you were in my skin, but you wouldn't know how to power through, how to outwit your oppressor, how to shake him off.'

'You don't look to me like someone on the path to freedom, you're nothing better than me,' concluded Uhunoma.

'How about we try something together?' suggested Amanda a little shyly.

Peals of laughter rang out from their cell—a true curiosity in the morning hours on the corridors of Bad Hallbach prison. There could be no doubt that anyone laughing with such sincerity in this place, at this time of day, could be anything but normal.

.34.

The prison was built in the early 20th century, but there were no recognizable stylistic features in its architecture. It was built functionally, one might even say progressively for the time when it was designed. The cells were spacious, unlike those in other prisons, the corridors airy, the building for the penitentiary had a record number of windows, and the guard towers shaped like medieval keeps with eaves were probably a kitschy flourish added by an imperial functionary whose taste had been formed at a Prussian military school. The imposing, perhaps even dignified appearance of the building gave everyone an unusual sense of safety: this told the prisoners they were in a dry, warm place, instead of in a penitentiary three times younger that was already crumbling, leaking when it rained and infested with insects, mice and rats; it sent a message to the prison officers and other personnel about the constancy of their goals. After all there are very few hundred-year-old buildings that still fulfil their primary function without significant renovation. The building had a goods lift and air vents. Only the old stable in the prison yard had been turned into a hall where the occasional prison performance was held.

Ebermaier strode down the corridor on the first floor of the prison. Four o'clock had passed and the doors to the cells were shut. He enjoyed this time of day when the inmates were locked again in their cells. Then he'd amble along the corridors and pop in to cells. Usually he had a plan for whom he was going to see and what he would do, but sometimes he'd ask the officer on duty on the floor to show him a list of the inmates and then he'd choose whom to visit based on the photograph by her name. There were often moments when he'd feel a sudden chill and ask himself whether one of these days he would have to answer for his behaviour. He wasn't thinking, of course, of earthly laws, but laws of the other realm. He hastily convinced himself that this was unlikely, because otherworldly laws, if they did, indeed, exist, had a higher purpose than dictating desirable behaviour in the cage known as human life. He was disgusted by all the primitive Catholic priests, his colleagues, who hypocritically sermonised about peace and love, and then in their sheds, monasteries or lavish flats, those who had them, they'd fornicate like beasts, sodomise boys, coerce girls, steal and cheat. He was prepared to answer to every authority and was braced to take the consequences: they, unlike him, were not. That is why he remained faithful to the habit, because he felt that the calling of the Catholic priest was truly God's mission on earth and only someone divinely chosen could be prepared to pay the price for his actions. Thousands of cowards all over the world called themselves Catholic priests, all were enthralled by their base passions, their frustrations and unfulfilled ambitions. That was Ebermaier's image of the Mother Church.

He was the one who had chosen the prison, nobody had sent him there, because the women prisoners know that society cares nothing for them: they have been relegated to the margins so they won't be an inconvenience. They know they are marked for life; there is no need to show them mercy. A firm hand is what they needed, someone who understood them and who would share with them the weight of the world. Ebermaier sometimes chuckled at his self-proclaimed messianism, he knew this was not what was going on. In fact, and this he often admitted candidly to himself, it was about his role, as mystical as it was attractive, as a man in a women's beehive. No matter how much they despised him, the women prisoners needed him, even lusted after him. Of course on the outside they never would have given him a second glance, but they were not on the outside, were they! They knew there was no liberty for them, and in this awareness lay their mutual attraction. Yes, call it perversion if you will, Ebermaier said to himself, but nobody lies here: I want their love and they want my power. As pastor to this flock, he knew everything about everyone: who was a drug smuggler, who was a neo-Nazi, who was a child-killer, and who a whore. And he secretly admired all of them: all these inmates, wherever they were from and wherever they were going, had their own moral codes and small, secret desires. And the humbler their desires, the more Ebermaier admired them. What made him the most powerful was the policy of the prison functionaries, dictating treatment that favoured them alone. This referred to every one of them, from the gate officer to the prison administration, and it included him. 'Are the tormentors in Dante's Hell sinners?' Ebermaier wondered with a twinge of irony before the officer let him into Uhunoma's and Amanda's cell.

When they heard the door being unlocked, Uhunoma and Amanda hopped onto their bunks. When he entered, he could see the two inmates, slightly out of breath, lying on their bunks. He didn't greet them, but tried to guess what had been going in the cell before he'd entered. Amanda interrupted his train of thought.

'Father, this little tart has something she wants to tell you.'

Ebermaier went over to her bunk, a little irritated that she had addressed him first, and pinched her cheeks as if to shut her up, though all Amanda had said was that one sentence. Amanda was pliant, so even while her face was being pinched she struggled to smile. Uhunoma felt fear. She knew how she was supposed to play, but she was uncomfortable even about her own decision to embark on this battle. Still she said what she'd agreed with Amanda to say, 'I think you should know that I am not HIV positive.' Ebermaier shot up to standing and stared at her in disbelief. Uhunoma expected Ebermaier would throw himself on her, but he just eyed her and tapped the floor with his toes.

Amanda deliberately broke the silence, saying, 'Father, believe her, this child does not know how to lie!' She laughed with a sickly sort of laugh that made Uhunoma queasy. Amanda ran her hand down Ebermaier's leg. Ebermaier brusquely pushed her away, turned towards the door and banging on it twice he summoned the officer.

When Ebermaier left, Amanda stood, went over to the door to listen to the priest's steps as he walked off, and whispered, 'Let's see if he has bitten.'

.35.

'Amanda Witherspoon,' thundered the voice over the loudspeaker. Uhunoma was still asleep and the abrasive voice of the head of shift who read announcements intended for individual cells sounded a lot like the cattle auction conducted over megaphone at the vast livestock market in Benin City. There, the main auctioneer, the most respected person at the fair, proudly held the megaphone, bringing it to his lips at a certain angle, as if addressing the gods instead of the buyers—villagers from the near and far reaches of the city. He was the unflappable king of the trade and nobody could touch him, though squabbles, and even bloody clashes, did, at times, erupt among the vendors. Uhunoma always stared, hypnotised by the auctioneer who was shouting into his megaphone, using an incomprehensible pidgin, pointing to the best offer at the end.

The person making the offer elbowed his way through the agitated, almost maddened, crowd, mounted the little stand fashioned of wooden crates and demanded to be taken to the herd. The owner of the herd also climbed up onto the stand, received the money from the buyer in front of everyone and then together they lead the herd some fifty metres away to the killing floor, where they select the cattle to be butchered immediately. The throng followed the entire process as if watching a performance. The herd numbered some thirty head of cattle and they were restless, because they sensed that something's coming. Still they obeyed orders while the dogs were always nipping at them to keep them in their groups. The buyer chose a dozen head of cattle and they were herded to the slaughter slab. The main butcher, in charge of all the butchering at the fair, came over to the cattle and chose the first one. Taking it by the horns he guided it over to the gutter for draining the blood from the slaughter slab, used deft movements to force it to kneel and lower its head, and then with his long, curved knife, reminiscent of a scimitar, he quickly cut its throat. The butcher kept holding the horns and aimed the bleeding at the gutter. The cow quickly collapsed, keeled over right at the start of the gutter, and died within a minute. Then the buyer's assistants climbed up onto the slaughter slab and started the butchering. The entranced throng pressed in closer, everyone wanted the finest cut of meat and, of course, the fresh offal. In a place where the temperature seldom drops below 27 degrees and where there is no point in owning a refrigerator because of the daily rolling blackouts, fresh meat is a major attraction. The auctioneer then assumed a new role. After conferring with the buyer, he began calling out the price of the meat over his megaphone for each part of the butchered animal and the throng began waving their wallets.

The voice over the loudspeaker said something in German and Uhunoma didn't understand it, but Amanda quickly jumped up from the bed, and while she was getting dressed she explained to Uhunoma, 'They are moving me again to another cell. They keep doing this. Who knows what Ebermaier said... Remember, this is your only chance, you must win over Ebermaier and persuade him to convince the police that the reporter is wrong. He can do that.'

The officers soon opened the door and led Amanda away. Uhunoma was left alone.

.36.

In the dining-hall, after a long time away, Uhunoma sat again with Sonja and Ivona. Uhunoma's appetite was back, and Sonja and Ivona had entered a more stable period of their relationship in which they were no longer afraid that somebody would discover them and they'd learned how to behave with decorum in public.

'Uhi, my dear, you look a fright!' said Sonja.

Indeed, Uhunoma's eyes and cheeks were sunken, her lips chapped and her hair tousled. Sonja and Ivona were hardly beauties, but they were managing well with what the prison psychologist referred to as the 'challenges of prison life.'

'Don't worry, everything is fine. Do you have any word about Nana?' asked Uhunoma.

'I've heard she is convalescing in hospital.' Sonja glanced over at Ivona with concern. 'But we actually don't know what is going on with her or what exactly happened to her.'

'You've heard she's convalescing?' Uhunoma was happy, forgetting for a moment where she was and all that was worrying her. 'I knew we'd all sit here together again at this table and listen to her wise stories.'

'It would seem we won't,' said Sonja.

'Why?'

'Because we are going to run away,' said Ivona.

'Where to?' asked Uhunoma.

'We don't care where we're going, just what we're running from. We will be escaping from here,' said Ivona resolutely.

'I am still trying to talk her out of this. I don't know where to go. Once I finish my sentence I'll decide what comes next.' Sonja was trying to weaken Ivona's resolve.

'How can you say such a thing?' Ivona said. 'I cannot bear to stay here any longer. I told you we'll easily reach Croatia, and then down to my folks in Herzegovina until the dust settles.'

'And when we come to your folks in Herzegovina, we'll be knocking at their door with our arms around each other? Things are only then likely to explode!'

Ivona was insistent. 'You'll be released before me, do you want me to wait for you? Will you wait for me, when you don't even know where you're going?'

'Listen, hon,' Sonja said, trying to calm her down,

'everything will be fine, don't you worry about a thing, Sonja will take care of you!' She pulled her close, and Ivona leaned her head on Sonja's shoulder.

'So what about you?' Ivona asked Uhunoma the question illegal immigrants cannot bear to hear. There is no time limit set for their stay in prison.

Sonja shot Ivona a reproachful glance, but Uhunoma quickly said, 'That's okay, Ivona, I don't know when I'll be released.'

Even if the women who are here as undocumented are, by some chance, released, they continue to be in violation of the law in most of the countries of Europe. Their status and residency will not have been resolved while they were in prison. Uhunoma went on to say: 'There are many people who spend a year in prison and then a month after they're released the police stop them and ask for identification and back they go to prison for yet another year. The thing is that after the year behind bars they should be deported back to their country, but if the government cannot send them back for whatever reason, and haven't managed to charge them, they must be released, though only until their next arrest.'

'Damned if you do, damned if you don't!' concluded Sonja.

'Well actually your situation is not so bad,' Ivona said, 'for me they know I'm Croatian. I had my passport with me. So they'll deport me either to Sarajevo or to

Zagreb. But when you tell them you're from Somalia or Sudan, they'll say—*nicht deportirung!*'

'Yes, true,' agreed Uhunoma, 'but I did not claim to be from Somalia or Sudan, and now they've fabricated charges against me using some story about human trafficking.'

'Wait, what? Who?'

'Father Ebermaier. Long story.'

'But why?' asked Ivona.

'Well actually I'm not sure. I will try to make friends with him, I have to convince him that I am in no way a threat.' Uhunoma laid out her plan to them in full.

'Uhi, this is an awful idea. Go see Cristina and ask her what to do. Don't give in to that vulture, he has fucked half the prison. What were you thinking?' Sonja took Uhunoma by the hand, literally pleading with her. Ivona pulled back from Sonja as if she'd been slapped in the face. Uhunoma noticed and withdrew her hand. Ivona jumped up and strode off, insulted, to her cell.

'Uhi, sorry, I have to go after her. Please, take care.'

Sonja jumped off and ran after Ivona. Uhunoma was left alone at the table to finish her lunch.

She went back to her empty cell. They didn't bring in anyone new. At first the cell felt large, larger than when it was shared by two, but within a few hours it shrank down to feeling much smaller, because instead of having her cellmate to look at, all she could look at were the walls, and instead of talking with someone, she talked with the walls and with herself.

Uhunoma spent the night alone, and it dragged by slowly, but somehow differently than before. She didn't feel such a powerful urge to get in touch with her parents in Nigeria. Through her fistfight with Amanda she'd found peace but also emptiness. She didn't know what the emptiness would bring her and she also didn't know how to deal with it. This was a new feeling and nobody had taught her about it or prepared her for it. She wanted to analyse it, establish what caused the condition and then somehow approach treating it, or at least repairing it. The old folk healer in her village always approached all his patients the same way, all illnesses too, and he'd find a medicine for each illness or pain. Once a man came to him whose HIV virus was active. He was growing weaker by the day and was certain he'd die. The healer asked him why he'd come if he was so sure he'd die. Everyone who heard what the healer said laughed at him, but they laughed because they weren't infected, at least they didn't know if they were or weren't. But the man was in no mood for laughing. He didn't even ask the healer for treatment. He turned and left and never returned. Soon the news reached the village that he had died. The healer gathered all those who would hear what he had to say—mostly children. He told them, 'That disease is the worst of all, death stole his every hope even before he'd died.' This was how she was feeling: her hope was utterly gone. She no longer felt a thing about the possibility that one day she'd walk, free, through the streets, nor that one day she might return to Nigeria. She needed Nana yet Nana wasn't there. She needed Nana to explain what was happening, but she wasn't there. She wasn't there.

.37.

Two, maybe three days went by. Uhunoma was no longer noticing the passage of time. The door was unlocked during the afternoon hours and in walked Ebermaier.

The door shut behind him, he went over to Uhunoma's bunk, and with an unusually easy-going look he said, 'I checked your prison file. You are, indeed, HIV negative. Congratulations!'

Uhunoma did not know how to respond. Ebermaier unbuttoned his shirt. She would have been happiest sending him packing. After her run-in with Amanda she'd become more confident of her strength and she had no doubt that it would take no more than a few moves to force him to capitulate. She could let him approach her without offering any resistance, then choose her moment when he was vulnerable, kneeing his balls as hard as possible. But that wasn't what she was after. She had to use the fact that the priest liked her to persuade him to convince the police that the charges raised against her were unfounded.

Ebermaier, bare to the waist, went over to Uhunoma's bunk. 'Come here,' he ordered her down to the lower bunk.

Uhunoma wavered. She came slowly down off her bunk, staying as far away as she could from where Ebermaier was standing. She balked at taking off her clothes. She thought about whether there was a way she could toy with Ebermaier so she wouldn't have to have sex with him. Ebermaier came to her first and took off her shirt. Her chance to play games was already history. She lost her will to do something. The priest began frantically kissing her breasts but she felt nothing, no pleasure and no disgust. He lay her down on the bed, undid her trousers and pulled them off. Uhunoma lay there, lifeless. He spread her legs, thrust into her and began what Uhunoma could recall from her distant past as sex. She was aware of the discomfort she was experiencing, but she buried it so deeply that Ebermaier's half-naked body rubbing against hers seemed like a machine running a sort of mechanical experiment on her, or maybe even performing a kind of treatment designed to erase the memories of everything that had ever been precious to her.

.38.

The days passed slowly and in them Uhunoma found peace. The seconds stretched, the minutes practically dissolved, and there were times when she felt as if the days had no beginning and no end. Waking up the morning after a troubled sleep was the only way to mark a new beginning, but a beginning for what—this she didn't know nor did she care.

The day was cloudy yet warm. You could go out into the prison yard in short sleeves, which was hardly typical for the Bavarian climate. After her walk around the yard, Uhunoma went back to her cell. As soon as she stepped inside, she was astonished: there was Nana on the lower bunk. She looked the same as she had before the heart attack—the dignified bearing, gentle smile, defiance and experience all mingling in her facial expression.

'Hello, Uhi,' said Nana. Uhunoma said nothing. 'Tortoise bit your tongue?'

Good old Nana, it truly was if she'd sprouted out of the prison wall, an endemic species, unadulterated, unchanged, having evolved into the bared obverse of prison life.

'Hey, Uhi, you're stronger than you pretend to be. Don't I at least get a hello? It's hardly my fault that I had a heart attack! I'd like to see how you shrinking violets would deal with cardiac arrest. I walked to the clinic, sat in a chair for half an hour until the on-duty doctor showed up, and he told me: 'You've had a heart attack'. Then an oxygen mask, the infirmary, medications, I had a marvelous rest. While you would have been trembling with fear, pleading for mercy, frantic about your fate. There is nothing, Uhi my dear, that you can change here. You can take care of yourself, yes, watch what you eat, get exercise, read, analyse your actions, you can do all of these things, but nothing will save you from the fear you feel. If you feel it.'

Uhunoma tried to laugh, but a smile simply wouldn't cross her face. It just simmered deep inside her, somewhere in the pit of her stomach. 'I no longer feel a thing, Nana,' she said.

'What is going on with you now?' Nana was curious.

Uhunoma said nothing for a moment before whispering, 'Ebermaier.'

'Oh no, Uhi,' Nana frowned, 'I knew you'd throw yourself into his jaws as soon as I left. But what could he offer you? Why did you give in to him?'

'Because of that reporter who claimed I was trafficking prostitutes.'

'Did he bring in the police?'

'I am not sure that he was the one who brought them in, but he did set it up.'

'And now he's fucking you?' Nana was furious.

'Yes.'

'You know what, I'll gouge his eyes out the first time he sets foot inside this cell!'

'Please don't, Nana, calm down, I need him so they don't take me to court and give me a longer sentence.'

'You are not in your right mind.' Nana jumped up and waved her arms around. 'Have you ever heard of a hunter helping his prey escape?'

'Nana, I have no choice.' Uhunoma forced a smile.

'Your life is on the line,' groaned Nana.

The next morning Nana went out into the corridor as soon as the cell door was opened. Uhunoma was lazing in bed, not yet fully awake. Nana quickly went downstairs towards the ground level and the cells where the German women were. If anyone had known that she'd had a heart attack only ten days before, they would have stopped and told her to slow down, because otherwise this wasn't going to end well. The door to Marta's cell was open and Nana almost ran in. Marta was sitting on the bed, watching a small battery-run television set.

'What's up, Kofi Annan?' Marta looked up, piercing Nana right away with the trite quip.

'Nothing, Adolf Hitler, I believe you must be aware of something.'

'Whoa, whoa, whoa!' Marta shouted. 'Don't you tell me, you piece of Ghanaian shit, that I am Hitler! For breakfast I eat Nazis. I don't hate nobody. I help you not because you black, but because you human! Come on, get out of my room!' Marta flew into a rage, and her shrill, raised voice sounded like an out-of-tune three-part harmony.

'Wait, Marta, I have something important to tell you, it's about Ebermaier,' said Nana, exuding courtesy.

'My Carlos?' Marta cooed the name of the priest who'd broken her heart and immediately looked sweetly up at Nana with a sort of mad light in her eyes.

'Yes, Carlos, about what he is up to with my cellmate.' Nana wanted to explain to Marta what was going on, but Marta already knew all about Ebermaier's past, current and future relationships.

'Ah, Carlos, he cannot function without *frische pussi*. Devil! He wants to try African woman. She has already fucked him?'

'Yes, Marta, she has,' said Nana.

'He is wild man, no heart,' said Marta sadly and scratched her double chin.

'You have to help me save Uhunoma from him,' Nana sad in an extremely conciliatory tone.

'Why?'

'Because she does not deserve this.'

'Stupid!' Marta laughed.

'Why are you laughing?' asked Nana, a little disappointed.

'Why you help the Nigerian woman? All they are thugs. Maybe you are honest, why believe her?'

'It doesn't matter whether I believe her, I feel bad for her.'

'What you want I do?'

'Tell Ebermaier to leave her alone.' Nana was firm.

'*Ich kann nicht*. You ask I defend a whore from my man. Won't go.'

'She is no whore. Ebermaier will destroy her. Think what he did to you! He used you when he needed you, when the daughter of that businessman reported him, you served as his screen.'

'Do not say that,' said Marta, 'he loved me and I him the same.' With each sentence Marta became more dispirited.

'You are the only one who can put a stop to this.' Nana grew very serious and looked into Marta's eyes.

'Good,' said Marta, absently, and turned back to the little television set.

.39.

Nana, Uhunoma and Sonja sat together again that day around a dining-hall table. Ivona was with them now, clinging to Sonja.

'What's up, kid, found your new boss?' Nana teased Ivona.

'Hey, old lady, cool it before you have another heart attack!' said Ivona, giggling, but no one else was laughing.

Sonja glared at her and Nana began tapping the table with her fingertips. Ivona's smile vanished, suddenly she even cringed, then, alarmed, she asked Sonja quite sheepishly in Croatian to tell her what she'd said wrong.

Sonja burst out laughing and hugged Ivona. First pretending to fend off the hug and protest the chicanery, though not too loudly, Ivona relented and gave Sonja a little kiss. Nana clapped.

'Uhi, things aren't so grim, we'll have fun, see,

we're not so bad off. Tell Ebermaier to fuck himself. I'll help. Right Nana?' Sonja was doing what she could to brighten the mood. Uhunoma was the only one who wasn't laughing.

Uhunoma found all this wearisome. She didn't want them to be laughing, she didn't want anyone reminding her of a state of mind in which you aren't torn between grief and remorse. She envied Sonja and Ivona their fresh romance and envied Nana her unswerving certitude. Who led her down this path? Poor parents who told her she had to start bringing earnings into the house when she was five, or maybe all those men who were always wanting to get their hands on her, or maybe it was simply a curse? She broke through the laughter around the table with a question for Ivona.

'Can your priests lift curses?'

Ivona glanced first at Sonja; she wasn't sure whether this was yet another joke on her account. Nana immediately cut through the anxiety.

'A Catholic priest cannot so much as kill his own louse, let alone lift a curse!' She turned to Uhunoma. 'You already have yourself a Catholic priest, have him lift curses? Are you crazy?'

Sonja interrupted. 'Hey, old lady, no point in rubbing it in. Why don't you give our friend here some advice, I would like to understand this sort of thing a little better, but sorry to say I never had the patience to listen to what my grandmother used to go on about when I visited her in the village a few times every year. Where I'm from in Serbia people sometimes died or disappeared, all from a curse.'

Ivona chimed in. 'Back home the priest would chase away demons if you asked him to come, welcomed him to the house, paid him something, too, but not a lot, you just had to be careful never to leave him alone in a room with a young girl possessed by a demon.'

'Why, so the demon wouldn't take him over?' asked Sonja.

'No, no, so the priest wouldn't go wild.'

Nana burst out laughing again, and Uhunoma got up from the table and went to the cell.

'Hey, old lady, you are pushing too hard.' Sonja blamed Nana for Uhunoma's bad mood.

'We mustn't give an inch,' answered Nana curtly, 'she got herself into this, now she must get herself out.' In a calmer tone, she added, 'Damn the curse that brought me into this world.'

Uhunoma walked toward her cell. Suddenly someone grabbed her by the shoulder from behind.

'I caught sight of you on the ground floor, but only caught up with you now. Why such a rush?' Ebermaier asked, out of breath, his face glowing.

Uhunoma wanted to shake him off, she did not

want him following her, all she needed was a little time to herself. Actually a lot of time to herself. 'I'm not feeling well. I can't eat.'

'I'm going with you, let me help you lie down.'

Uhunoma recognised the priest's intentions, and as if what she had just said had come true, she really did begin to feel ill. She was overcome with the shakes, and if Ebermaier hadn't grabbed her by the arm, she would have slumped to the cold cement floor of the corridor. Although she could barely walk, Ebermaier dragged her from the second to the third floor, all the way to her cell. He shoved her in, she fell to her knees, and he quickly tore off his clothes. Uhunoma crawled over to the toilet bowl and vomited into it. She didn't even have the time to wipe her mouth when Ebermaier grasped her from behind by the hips, pulled down her pants and began his by now familiar sexual routine. He moaned as he climaxed, and then stood up abruptly, rinsed his penis off in the sink, pulled on his clothes and went out into the corridor.

Uhunoma thought he was gone, but the next moment the door opened again and Ebermaier tottered in backwards, falling across Uhunoma's half-naked body. Marta, who could hardly fit through the door and had barely enough room to turn around in the small cell, shoved him in. Marta was holding a length of sawed-off lead pipe and Ebermaier pleaded with her in German.

'Marta, darling, don't!'

Marta smacked him on the head and Ebermaier fell to the floor next to Uhunoma, who was struggling to register what was going on. Then Marta hit him a few more times on his back, not as hard, with the lead pipe. After that she spat on him, swore something garbled and left the room.

.40.

Ebermaier rose slowly and was only just able to scramble to his feet. He wanted to run after Marta, but his head was spinning and his back hurt so badly that he couldn't fully straighten up. Uhunoma watched him from where she lay. Only moments ago he had been a powerful, potent figure, and now above her stood a wounded, doddering old man, who looked as if he might collapse and die. Saliva mixing with blood dribbled from his mouth. One of his arms jerked as if he couldn't control it. He needed a few minutes to make his way out of the small cell, while stumbling, grabbing the bed, leaning on the wall, struggling the whole time to breathe, spraying around him a fine mist of bloody droplets.

The next morning Nana went out onto the corridor again as soon as the door was opened and quickly came back in with news of how the situation was developing. After they'd learned what had happened the day before, Sonja and Ivona also came to Uhunoma and Nana's cell. The three women sat on the floor around Uhunoma who was lying on Nana's bunk.

'Marta will be taken today to another prison which has a far stricter regimen for movement than ours does. She'll go to trial for attempted murder. This was her second time. What will we do with you?' Nana's question was intended more for Sonja and Ivona than for Uhunoma who was staring blankly at the upper bunk.

'Uhi, why didn't you fight back? Why didn't you bash him over the head with this?' Nana pointed to the broken toilet seat which was propped up against the wall next to the toilet.

'Did he... again?' Sonja asked, but Nana indicated with a nod that she shouldn't say anything more.

'Have you showered since what happened yesterday?' asked Nana calmly.

'How could I? I have been here the whole time,' answered Uhunoma listlessly.

'Okay, then arise, oh army, off we march to the infirmary!' shouted Nana.

'Why?' Uhunoma didn't feel like getting up.

'So the on-duty doctor can take a sample from your cunt and figure out whose semen is in there!'

Ivona protested. 'You're crazy! You'll all be put in

isolation, the priest will bury you all alive, Sonja, let's get out of here.'

'*Ne mrdaj!*' barked Sonja in Serbian. 'Don't you budge! We're staying here!'

'*Kurvo glupa!*' said Ivona. 'Stupid whore! ' Their spat went on in the language only the two of them understood. 'Let's not draw attention to ourselves. Tomorrow I am on the roster for a visit to the supermarket and you know what that means.'

'Fuck that, Uhi is falling apart here, escape some other time!'

'You are not in your right mind. You'd leave me in the lurch to help these bitches. Pitiful. Fuck off!' Ivona ran out of the cell.

Sonja stayed in the cell and helped Nana persuade Uhunoma to go down with them to the infirmary. Everyone looked at them as they slowly made their way along the corridors, Uhunoma in the middle, Sonja and Nana supporting her on each side. When they reached the barred door on the ground floor separating the area where the prisoners lived from the rest of the prison, Nana shouted, at the top of her lungs, 'Open the door!'

Several officers came running over, and asked Nana, 'What are you shouting for?'

'This prisoner has been bleeding for two days and she refuses to see the doctor,' said Nana in fluent German, while pointing to Uhunoma. 'If you don't let her into the infirmary, she may bleed to death.'

'Come on, hurry.' The female officer in charge let them into the ground-floor reception area and signalled to the male officer on the other side of the door to open it. 'You stay here,' she said, gesturing to Sonja, blocking her way.

Three female officers moved Uhunoma and Nana speedily along to the infirmary in the eastern wing of the building. They passed through several locked and barred gates and doors until they reached the on-duty doctor's consulting room. The doctor was at his desk, reading a large book. Nana and Uhunoma could see him through the open office door as he smoked and jotted notes down in a small notebook.

At the prompting of one of the officers he stood up and came, reluctantly, into the consulting room. 'What seems to be the problem?' he said, donning his eyeglasses. He was in his forties, with a slightly loutish expression and a scar over his upper lip.

'Order the army to withdraw, every patient has the right to privacy,' said Nana as if she were the one issuing commands.

'Ha, ha, clever one, and who are you two, the Queen of Sheba and her handmaiden?' The doctor lit another cigarette.

'Perhaps we are,' answered Nana, 'but that is neither here nor there. So, doctor, how will this go, will you tell your Amazons here to leave us alone or not?' Nana crossed her arms and Uhunoma slipped her hand under Nana's.

'That is against the rules,' said one of the female officers who was following the conversation between the doctor and Nana.

The doctor eyed the female officer, stepped over to his desk in the consulting room, then briefly rummaged in the drawer for his surgical instruments, making a lot of noise in the process, and finally victoriously produced a small scalpel. 'Now we can,' he said and gestured with the scalpel for the officers to wait out in the hall.

'As you wish,' said the officer and left the consulting room with the other two.

'I was hoping I wouldn't encounter the doctor who received me here when I had the heart attack,' said Nana to Uhunoma, but loudly enough that the doctor also heard her.

'I don't know what you two are up to, but you should know that I am a surgeon and I know exactly where to stab you with this scalpel so that the two of you knock at heaven's door in a matter of seconds.'

The doctor stood by his desk, still smiling but his smile was strained. Brash Nana and broken Uhunoma gave the impression they had walked there straight from hell. They might be addicts, child-killers, HIV-ers, prostitutes out to turn a trick from inside prison, and the doctor had no idea what had brought them to him.

'Were you on duty yesterday afternoon?' Nana asked him, still with her resolute, commanding tone.

'No, I was not. I came on duty early this morning.'

'Do you know whether the prison chaplain was brought in here yesterday afternoon?'

'I know one of the inmates beat him up.' The doctor was a little alarmed. 'Listen, that is none of my business, if she was your friend, I have nothing to do with it, I am only doing my job. It's best that you go right back to your cells and nobody will suffer the consequences.'

'Listen, that same priest sexually abused this young woman repeatedly. Please, examine her and take a sample of his semen. It is still inside her.'

'Good try, whores,' said the doctor, fingering his scalpel. 'You give a blow job to an innocent man, and then rub his sperm into your cunt and accuse him of rape. Get out! Get lost!' he shouted.

The female officers came back and pushed Uhunoma and Nana out into the hall. While they were escorting them back to the central part of the building, Uhunoma started crying. The officers told her to shut up and pushed her to speed her up. Nana didn't want to say a word and held herself upright the whole way, though the officers lashed her with insults and said they were in big trouble now.

When the officers brought them to the big door toward the wing with the cells, Uhunoma began to scream, 'I don't want to go back. I don't want to go back. Let me go! Let me go!'

The officers were about to drag her through the door but Nana jumped to protect her. The officers separated them: one brought Uhunoma in, while the other two brought in Nana, who was much stronger and more belligerent. The left them on the ground floor, on the other side of the main door. Sonja was no longer there in the hallway so the two of them, heads bowed, went back to their cell.

After the cell door was locked that afternoon, Nana promised Uhunoma: 'Nobody will touch you here any more.'

.41.

The governor appeared to speak to the inmates in person for the first time that anyone at the prison could remember. The day was lovely and dry and most of the population was brought out to the yard before lunch. Uhunoma, Nana and Sonja stood by the wall. The governor used a megaphone to speak to the crowd from the window of the administrative building. His soporific tone was familiar to all of them, but the more short-sighted among them couldn't make out whose head it was at the window on the third floor. This time the governor spoke in slow English.

'Dear inmates, this is governor Steiner speaking. I am very disappointed to report that for the first time in six years we have had an inmate escape from one of our prison units. Most of you know the identity of the fugitive. The day before yesterday in the afternoon, this inmate left the prison unit on the regular, approved visit to the local supermarket. When crossing the road at the traffic light the inmate ran off into the town of Bad Hallbach. The officers, keeping in mind my recommendation that one mustn't shoot at an escapee in an inhabited area, pursued the inmate. However she was running extremely fast and after she'd gone beyond the first corner, they lost all trace of her. The police search was called off this morning and the blockade of Bad Hallbach was lifted. The inmate was not apprehended. But you can be sure that she will soon be back at Bad Hallbach correctional institution or another facility in the federal prison system. She does not have much choice, for now she has made the worst choice of all the choices available to her. The inmate came to Germany from, just a moment...' The governor had to ask an official standing next to him for the information. 'Yes, from Bosnia and Herzegovina. Do you think she'll return to Bosnia and Herzegovina? No, she will not. Otherwise she wouldn't have come here in the first place. She will remain in Germany, and perhaps she will go even farther to the west. Because of our tolerant border regime and the lenient system she will evade the law for a time, but living a life without the proper documents she is quite likely to commit another misdemeanour, more than likely the same one that brought her here before. Then she will be sent back to us with a longer prison sentence, depending on the crime she committed while a fugitive. And, in the end, what will she have achieved?'

'She will never come back!' shouted Sonja in English as loudly as she could. Suddenly the entire crowd, who had stood by quietly until then, began milling around, shouting, cursing, and gesticulating at the governor's window.

'Quiet please, quiet,' said the governor, 'you won't be given lunch if you don't quiet down,' and then repeated this in German. Having heard his threat, the inmates obeyed.

'I advise you to follow prison rules and please keep in mind that you must respect them because of the impact your behaviour may have on the whole community. This correctional institution is a small community of its own. And because of this inmate's escape, our facility will be removed from the federal programme for low-security prisons. It will take us five years to enter the programme again. And had we stayed in the programme, as soon as next year each inmate would have had the right to go into town once a month, escorted by police and social workers, participate in workshops with inmates in Ulm, and many other programmes. Five years, remember that. The choice is yours.'

The governor withdrew from the window and out in the prison yard there was instant pushing and shoving as people competed to see who would be first to go back in to the dining-hall for lunch. Uhunoma saw a tiny woman weeping as she sank to the ground in despair.

After lunch, Uhunoma was ready to go back to her cell.

'Wait, Uhi,' said Nana while the three of them were still at the dining-hall table. 'Do you think Ivona has someone to go to nearby? Is it possible that the little bird came up with a proper plan?'

'Unlikely,' said Sonja. 'What a stupid fuck, and what the hell is she going to do now, whatever did she need to do that for?'

'Everything will be fine,' said Uhunoma.

Sonja and Nana sat up, as if a dead person had spoken.

'You're coming back to us, Uhi!' Nana was pleased. 'Come on, Sonja, let's go watch television, that will cheer you up.'

'In the room with all the German women?' asked Sonja.

'Of course. Why? Are you afraid of them?' Nana teased.

'No, but they watch programs in German and I can't understand a word. You know, like, there's Brad Pitt but he's speaking German and that kind of shit.'

'Who cares, let's go enjoy ourselves for a few minutes. When did you last watch television, Uhi?'

'I can't remember,' said Uhunoma.

Sonja, Uhunoma and Nana took seats on the wooden chairs in the lounge where a dozen women were watching a show in German—a talk show with guests in the studio. Sonja, Uhunoma and Nana were entranced by the clothing and make-up worn by the people in the studio, the glamour of the stage set, and most of all they were overwhelmed by the jarring advertisements: in a perfectly outfitted kitchen full of gaudy, unnatural and sterile colours, a little boy was eating a slice of chocolate cake with his fingers and he had chocolate smeared all over him. His face was smudged with chocolate and he was grinning from ear to ear. There was chocolate icing on his shirt, trousers, even his little trainers. The mother caught him just as he was swallowing the last crumb of cake. She was furious. The German women in the first row commented, 'Come on, Mum, don't be a cow, now, give the boy more cake!' All the Germans laughed, and one added, 'I'd like to see you, Mum, if you were alone in the room with that cake!' A toothless old woman among them cracked a smile and declared, 'My mother didn't stop me from eating cakes and look at me now!' The girl sitting next to her laughed so hard she fell off her chair and the other women went on laughing at her clumsiness.

'Wait, wait,' said Uhunoma, because suddenly Ursula Heinz appeared on the screen, and the background behind her showed a picture of Bad Hallbach prison. 'There's that reporter.'

'Come on, Nana, translate,' said Sonja.

The German women also listened tensely, once they realised that what they were watching was a report on their prison.

Nana listened with her head bowed and finger raised, meaning she was listening closely and they mustn't disturb her while she was concentrating on the rapid German Heinz used on the small screen attached to the wall. Uhunoma suddenly heard Ursula Heinz giving her name.

'Why is she mentioning me?' she asked Nana.

Nana held her finger in the air for a few more seconds, and then she turned to Sonja and Uhunoma. 'I am sorry, Uhi, the reporter has referred to you as a dangerous criminal who is hiding in our prison, using a false identity.'

Uhunoma looked at Sonja and Nana and said, 'I am done for. I'll be stuck in prison forever. Wow, am I fucked.'

Sonja was silent, but Nana as always, had an answer at the ready. 'Listen to me closely, Uhi. Yes, you are in deep shit, but you'll manage. First they'll charge you, then take you to court, and in the end the court will free you for lack of evidence. Do not confess to anything they're trying to frame you with. Do not say anything to them but the truth. If you try to dodge, to evade, you'll come across as unreliable. Stay with the truth, tell them about every single croissant you pickpocketed at Lidl's, each time you dodged a bus fare, each time you jaywalked. And tell them what Ebermaier did to you here. Tell them, let them investigate. They'll assign you some asshole lawyer who won't even know how to pronounce your name properly, but be patient and guide the lawyer with instructions from the start about what to say. He'll object at first but soon he'll go along with your plan, because that will be much easier for him. He won't have to strategize. Got it?'

All the German women wandered out of the lounge, as the time neared for returning to the cells. Nana and Sonja stood at the door to the room and Uhunoma was still sitting on the chair, staring at the screen where a documentary on the Grand Canyon was starting.

'Come on, Uhi, otherwise they'll be shooing us into our cell,' said Nana.

'Leave her be, we have another twenty minutes,' said Sonja. 'Look, Uhi, I'll show you something that might interest you.' Sonja sat down again next to Uhunoma and from the back pocket of her prison trousers she took out a slip of paper that had been folded and refolded.

'What is that?' asked Uhunoma.

'My petition for conditional release,' said Sonja.

'My, my, so who is getting ready to leave us?' Nana wanted to know.

'Unfortunately, not me,' laughed Sonja and smoothed out her tattered piece of paper, 'but I keep it with me. I find it poignant.'

'How can you find a petition for conditional release poignant, especially one that has been denied?' Nana was surprised.

'Here, take a look and see if you can figure out why.' Sonja gave her the petition.

Nana read aloud, '*Anwendung für die Bewährung*, Application for conditional release, and what is this third language marked SK?'

'Serbokroatisch,' answered Sonja, 'the German abbreviation for the language I speak.'

'So what does this say here?' asked Nana.

'Below it says my petition has been denied. Those are the only words I can read in my language. Here, look, Uhi, look what it says down at the bottom.' Sonja took the petition from Nana and gave it to Uhunoma.

Uhunoma read, also aloud, and sounded out the German: '*Entlassung verweigert bis...*' wait, your release has been denied for the next five years?' Sonja listened, stone-faced. Nana said not a word. They went off toward their cells.

.42.

It is morning. Even in a quiet prison where everyone is following house rules and where at lunchtime you can hear the officers marching by during the shift change, even there the silence first thing in the morning is special. Night may be quiet, but the darkness interferes with your reliance on sight and makes your hearing sharper. You can hear the cockroaches chewing on the crumbs that dropped from your bread roll, the cough of the officer on duty several floors below, a train passing in the distance—all of this is a kind of noise. But in the morning, at dawn, your sight awakens and you see: your sight dulls your hearing and for a time you watch the ray of sunlight on the cell wall, you follow the shadow of the bed as it moves with the rising of the sun, you are awed by the colours you can see again, as they emerge from the dark. And you don't hear a thing.

'Uhunoma Ahano!' suddenly boomed from the loudspeaker in the cell. 'Pack up your things and prepare to come down to the front gate!'

Nana shot awake and peered upward towards Uhunoma who had greeted the dawn, leaning on her elbows. A second later a small smile crept onto her lips. 'Is that you they're calling, girl? It went by fast, I have to say!'

'What went by fast?' huffed Uhunoma unhappily and sat up.

She couldn't see Nana's face but she clearly heard Nana say, 'You're moving on... What was far away is now near.'

Uhunoma sensed a note of melancholy in Nana's voice and only then did she realise why they were summoning her over the public address system. Nana was ahead of her again.

'There are no visitors this early in the day. Your time is up, my dove, off you go.'

Uhunoma climbed down from the bunk and squinted through the tall window of the cell as if to ascertain just what time it really was.

'Come on, you don't have much time. Get ready, don't forget anything.'

Anticipation and sadness fought inside Uhunoma. She wanted to tell Nana how excited she was, she wanted to tell her she was scared, she didn't want to go, really, she wished she could stay.

'We'll see each other again.'

Nana didn't give her time to think. She sprang to her feet and started gathering Uhunoma's belongings. Uhunoma knew she'd never see Nana again, her throat clenched and her heart began to pound.

'Hey, kid, hold your head up high, brace yourself for the worst, and—off we go!'

Nana handed her the toiletries that were scattered around the little cell. Uhunoma tucked her things into a plastic bag. She knew what lay ahead of her: transfer to a new prison, or if they did drop the charges, then deportation to Africa. The door was unlocked and two officers were standing outside in the corridor. '*Toalette*,' said one and pointed to the toilet. Uhunoma understood, crouched over the toilet and pulled up her nightie. And indeed, as if the body found it easier to obey than think autonomously, her urine gushed out in a powerful stream.

'You're off on a journey, so be it,' said Nana, and laid her hand on Uhunoma's shoulder. Uhunoma wanted to hug her but didn't. She didn't want to believe she was really leaving. Who would move into Nana's cell? Would Nana look after the new cellmate the way she'd looked after Uhunoma? Can anyone anywhere in the world be so generous, so calm and so kind? She might have hugged her if the officers hadn't been prodding her to get dressed: leave the nightgown on the edge of the bed, strip the bunk and throw the bedding in the corner of the cell, lift the mattress for check, fine, hand over her plastic bag for a check, okay, let's go. The cell door closed and Nana stayed behind it.

Uhunoma went through another physical, this time in preparation for departure. Again you strip, and fat and thin female crones pat down your body, peer into your rectum, push a finger up your vagina, sniff your clothing, wearing gloves the whole time and reminding you of butchers. Normal procedure. The male officers at the inner gate look just as lazy as when you arrived, again they don't look you in the eye, they sigh while they speak. They look as if they'd let you walk away if only that wouldn't compromise their jobs. You realise that this moment, leaving for a transfer to another correctional institution is one of the high points of prison life. Everyone is glad you're going, you are no longer a burden for them, and you are glad, you'll spend another few hours in a small armoured van, which, in comparison to the hundreds of tons of brick walls and dozens of prison officers, seems so inconsequential. All that stands between you and freedom is a thin metal door. But you can ignore it because you're being taken through streets where other free people are travelling alongside you and you're looking up at the same sky that they see.

ACKNOWLEDGEMENTS

This book would never be finished if not for the generous patience of my wife Osas and our sons Stanko and Amadin. My Croatian editor Nenad Popović takes credits for encouraging me to believe in what I wanted to write. Ten years later the book is coming out in the language the characters spoke in my head while I was writing the novel. This happened because of a great help and friendship of Ellen Elias Bursać, Buzz Poole and Onyeka Nwelue.

www.ingramcontent.com/pod-product-compliance
Lightning Source LLC
Chambersburg PA
CBHW030820210726
48290CB00002B/686